THE RAKE'S CONVENIENT BRIDE

MADELINE MARTIN

Cover Design by Wicked Smart Designs

Published by Oliver-Heber Books

0 9 8 7 6 5 4 3 2 1

PROLOGUE

Oh, how Lady Elizabeth Ashbrook hated resolutions for the new year. Those promises to better oneself were a source of turbulent frustration. At least to her.

Perhaps if she could control her own actions, they would not be so loathsome. But when one's faults stemmed from being clumsy, how was one supposed to endeavor to be fixed?

Elizabeth couldn't exactly wish away the various pavement cracks, loose nails, or errant drips from her life.

And yet here she was, amid her dearest friends just after the daunting chime of midnight, with their resolutions hanging over them like something heavy and ominous.

Hannah held the journal in her hands, her cheeks flushed almost as red as her hair with excitement to record all their intentions for self-improvement. She glanced at Lucy's empty bed and smothered a laugh. "Clearly, Lucy's resolution will not be punctuality."

Elizabeth joined the others in a good-natured giggle. Lucy was always running late. Not due to a lack of attention, but due to a lack of care.

Lucy was bold like that. Confident to the point of being enviable. Never in her life did Lucy seek approval or care if the rules were being followed.

Perhaps it was why of the five, Elizabeth was closest with Lucy.

Where Lucy was carefree, Elizabeth was obsequious, following rules within every narrow line and margin. Where Lucy took chances, Elizabeth stayed within the confines of expectation and propriety. Where Lucy was a vibrant of character, Elizabeth was dull—shy, quiet, and demure.

Perhaps Elizabeth's resolution ought to be to allow herself to become more like Lucy.

But no, for all intents and purposes, Elizabeth was doing what she should be by the standards set for an earl's eldest daughter. Emulating Lucy would not improve her character. Not to the outside world, at least.

"Maybe she's with Lady Alison, selecting ribbons for class." Jillian pinned her dark waves with a pinch of her fingers as if it were a bow, innately artistic with the deft movement of her fingers. She gave a wry twist to her lips and rolled her eyes.

The very idea of Lucy spending a moment of time with the likes of Lady Alison was preposterous.

Hannah erupted into laughter, the clear bell of her mirth ringing out in the small room. If Lucy was vibrant, Hannah was incandescent. Her voice was always the loudest in the room, her joy uninhibited in a way that always brought a smile to Elizabeth's lips.

Hannah clapped her hand over her mouth, her eyes wide, as though the volume had surprised even her.

But Lucy *was* taking a terribly long time. She'd vowed to bring a treat to make the resolution party memorable. It didn't take much to deduce she likely intended to smuggle the bit of brandy that old Jones kept hidden behind the sofa.

"Hopefully she didn't take a tumble." Elizabeth looked toward the closed door, earnestly regretting having told Lucy about the stash of liquor in the first place. The poor harassed butler was always pausing by the immensely pink and frilly sofa. He went so often, in fact, it did not take long for Elizabeth to catch him slugging back a draught from the bottle one afternoon amid his irascible grousing about the girls and their antics.

What good could possibly have come from divulging such a secret to Lucy?

"I'll wager she's up to no good." Amy frowned, her maternal side matching that of Elizabeth's concern. But then, the two of them had always been the ones to look after the others. Elizabeth, from a place of imagining every catastrophe that could befall those she cared about, spurred on by her own impossible clumsiness, and Amy, from a place of craving the warmth of a family.

She would make an excellent mother someday with all that love and care in her heart.

Hannah giggled and pointed to Amy's head where her silky blonde hair was tied up in rag rolls that bobbed about when she spoke.

Before Amy could chide Hannah, the door swung open and Lucy sauntered in, a triumphant smile on her lips. She tossed her head back to clear a lock of dark hair from her hazel eyes and grinned at them. "I thought our resolutions could be a little more interesting." From behind her back, she withdrew a corked bottle.

Elizabeth had been correct. Poor Jones would find his

secret stash nearly empty the next morning, if not gone entirely.

Hannah leapt to her feet, abandoning that journal Elizabeth loathed so greatly, and ran toward Lucy with a high-pitched squeal.

"I don't think we should have that." Even as Amy spoke cautiously, she slid from her bed to examine the brandy bottle.

"From ol' Jones's private stash that he keeps behind the sofa." Lucy wiggled the bottle, sending the liquid sloshing about. "And don't fret…" She looked pointedly at Elizabeth. "I left him a few coins to cover a new bottle of an even finer vintage than this."

And this is why Lucy was so easy to envy. Despite her carelessness, there was still a deep consideration for others. One that sometimes made Elizabeth wonder if Lucy was truly as indifferent as she appeared—or if it was all a ruse for something deeper.

Elizabeth beamed her approval at Lucy, winning a proud smile from her friend in return.

"How much does it take to get drunk?" Jillian asked, peering curiously at the bottle.

Lucy pulled the cork free and the hollow thunk filled the room. "We'll find out." She sniffed the contents, but despite her bravado, a look of disgust pulled at her features. "I imagine it won't be much." Acting on impulse, as she was wont to do, she put the bottle to her lips and tilted her head back. She swallowed, grimaced, and lowered the brandy as she wheezed out a pained exhale.

"I think you're supposed to sip it," Jillian mused.

"I've never been a rule-follower," Lucy ground out, likely

trying to salvage her brave demeanor. She passed the bottle to Hannah. "And neither have you."

Hannah hesitated, her head tilted in a show of skepticism. "I ought to take offense to that."

"But you won't," Lucy replied, her husky voice restored.

Hannah didn't bother to protest—or hesitate—and put the rim to her lips and took a swig as hearty as Lucy's.

Her blue eyes bulged, and her face went deep red right up to the roots of her hair. Features contorting in agony, she swallowed, the sound making an audible gulp before she exhaled a pained wheeze.

Amy rushed to Hannah's side, patting her back, concern evident in her wide, dark-brown gaze.

For her part, Elizabeth wanted nothing to do with the stuff. Save it for Jones in her opinion. He clearly had greater need of it than they.

"Is the taste really that bad?" Elizabeth asked, knowing she'd likely be coerced into taking a sip as well despite her unwillingness to do so.

She was spared from being next when Jillian pried the bottle from Hannah's clutched fist, the challenge making that glint show in Jillian's eyes. She put the rim to her lips, drank deeply and shrugged. "Not bad."

Elizabeth gaped at her.

All at once, Jillian burst into a sputtering laugh that turned into a gagging cough, her blue eyes brilliant as they watered. "But not good either," she rasped.

Amy ran to her and gently thwacked at her back until Jillian waved her off, still laughing.

"Let's get to our resolutions before any one of us has to

drink more of that." Jillian pointed an accusatory finger at the brandy.

The tension knotting at Elizabeth's shoulders eased somewhat, and she gave Jillian a grateful smile.

Her friend winked back in understanding. Of the five, Elizabeth and Amy were the least adventurous. Jillian was inclined to allow people to do as they please without compulsion. But then, with all the pressure her own parents had applied on her through her life, it was no wonder.

There was something free and beautiful about Jillian. Not in the rebellious way like Lucy, who seemed ready to throw her actions in the face of those who challenged her. No, Jillian wanted to do what she wanted to for her sake alone, to appease some pulse within her that thrummed to a different beat than others.

Elizabeth envied Jillian as well, the confidence of knowing and accepting herself so thoroughly.

Lucy tucked the bottle against her arm, and they gathered closer to the hearth while Hannah collected the journal.

The plush, salmon-colored carpet was warm in front of the hearth, heating the chill in Elizabeth's limbs. All eyes turned to her, and she swallowed down her anxiety. Or at least some of it.

Amy carefully dipped the quill in ink for her, likely so Elizabeth wouldn't spill it.

Dread tightened in her stomach. Might as well declare her resolution now and get the whole business of it over with.

"I vow to be less clumsy this year," Elizabeth announced. "Or at least not be so terribly awkward about it."

Amy cast her a sympathetic look and passed the prepared quill.

Elizabeth readily accepted the journal to avoid seeing the pity on their faces. '1810' was written with immaculate perfection in Amy's neat script. Elizabeth added her resolution in a carefully neat hand, in an effort to match the elegance of her friend's writing.

Miss Cuthbert would likely be pleased with both of them for such penmanship.

"And you, Amy?" Hannah asked.

Amy accepted the book from Elizabeth and gently blew at the page to dry the ink. "I would like to always be kind."

"You are always kind," Lucy groaned and gave her a grimace of exasperation.

Even Amy rolled her eyes at this, albeit playfully, and carefully wrote her resolution.

"And I resolve…" Lucy tossed back another gulp of brandy with barely a wince this time.

"To be as wicked as possible," they all finished for her in chorus.

Elizabeth laughed aloud and the other three girls joined her.

Lucy blinked in surprise, mock offense showing dramatically on her features. "Apparently I ought to resolve to be less predictable."

Elizabeth grinned at her friend, loving seeing her boldness in its full glory. "Don't you dare. We'd be at a loss as to what to do with you."

Lucy gave a throaty laugh and drank from the bottle again.

Elizabeth glanced toward Hannah as Lucy wrote her resolution in the journal.

A look of apprehension crossed Hannah's face, and she sighed. "To be more patient."

"Isn't that what you tried last year?" Amy asked gently.

Lucy scoffed. "And only made it a week last year, if I recall."

Hannah wrinkled her nose. "To be fair, patience does take a while." Twisting her lips to the side, she took the book from Lucy and began to write in a slow, careful, evidently patient script.

As they'd all given their resolutions, Jillian was clearly next.

Elizabeth sat a little straighter in anticipation. One never knew what to expect with Lady Jillian Jennings. The only girl of five children, spoiled to a fault as a child, and then the reins tightened on every aspect of her life once she was old enough to declare she wanted to be an artist instead of an earl's daughter. As a result of such freedom, followed by such restraint, with a head filled with dreams and feet that refused to stay on the ground, she was perfectly unpredictable.

"I resolve…" She swept her finger over the page as if she expected magic to secret her the answer. "To never wed."

The girls all sucked in a breath. Well, except Lucy, who simply smirked.

Surely they had not heard correctly. Elizabeth gaped at Jillian. "What?"

"What if none of us ever wed?" Jillian's chin lifted slightly, and she got that dreamy look on her face like when an idea struck her. "We wouldn't have to cede ourselves or our property to a man, we wouldn't be forced into an uncomfortable match."

"I don't want to wed either," Lucy said firmly, her resolution thrown into the group like betting chips in a card game.

"Perhaps we could all live on a country estate together

when we become spinsters and our parents have given up on us," Jillian mused. "And we can make the ballroom into an extra library, stacked to the ceiling with books."

Elizabeth's pulse quickened. An extra library. Stacked to the ceiling with books. And no obligation to think of. Just day after glorious day in the country with no balls to attend or dinners to fret over. No stiff, uncomfortable gowns she had to worry about staining, or men she would have to parade in front of to impress while hoping not to trip. Just Elizabeth and books and the idea of reading uninterrupted for days, weeks, months, *years* on end.

And maybe they could even have a music room where they could host their own concerts. After all, Jillian did play the most exquisite harp, and Elizabeth had always wanted to learn the flute.

"I shouldn't like to wed, either." Hannah grabbed the bottle from Lucy and slugged back a drink, as if sealing the pledge with the burn of alcohol.

A smile brightened Jillian's face as she wrote on a fresh page—*The Vow of the Wallflowers,* with the 's' blooming into a perfectly drawn rose. She signed, then passed the journal to Lucy who did likewise, and then on to Hannah.

Elizabeth nearly grabbed the book, but hesitated.

She had two younger sisters, both of whom would need to see Elizabeth married before their own chances for unions could be considered. But the thought of meeting men, worrying about treading on their feet or falling on the dance floor, of humiliating someone by spilling something on herself—or worse, on them—it was all too much.

She would never be good enough for love—why bother even trying?

"No man wants a wife who trips over air." Elizabeth pushed aside her doubt and reached for the book. "And I should love a music room filled with every instrument I could play regardless of the time." She gave a firm nod. "I'm in too."

It wasn't until after Elizabeth signed the book that she considered Amy.

Poor, sweet Amy, with her cheeks brilliant red and a look of hopeless shock in her large brown eyes. Her mouth opened, and closed, and opened again.

Elizabeth shook her head, not wanting her friend to sign. Amy was destined to be a mother, pouring all that love she had into children who would adore her with equal measure.

"You don't have to sign," Hannah said, echoing Elizabeth's own sentiments.

Amy squared her shoulders. "And abandon you lot of spinsters in that manor without someone to properly look after you?" She reached for the book and added her own signature, one she had practiced to loopy perfection. "Besides, I should like to bake confections in a kitchen without judgement."

"Then it is done." Jillian snapped the book closed, sat back on her heels, and beamed at them all. "None of us will ever marry."

"Wallflowers to the end," Hannah declared triumphantly and took one final swig from the bottle.

And so it was…their fates were sealed.

1

FEBRUARY 1817, LONDON, ENGLAND

*E*lizabeth held the leather journal in her hands, that
blasted book from all those years ago when she and
her friends—who affectionately referred to themselves as the
wallflowers—had vowed to never marry.

Except now Hannah was not only wed, but also in a delicate way, and Elizabeth had drawn the bit of paper declaring
she was next to break the oath.

Of course, Hannah had looked radiant with her skin
glowing with good health and her eyes bright with undeniable
happiness, hand resting on her swollen middle, as though she
could caress the child within.

Elizabeth did not want that life, one with children she
would embarrass and a husband who would likely roll his
eyes at her clumsiness.

But her friends were not the only ones who had an eye
toward Elizabeth finally marrying. Her sisters had been
nattering on for the last three hours about a ball being held by
Lady Gentry, her first of the season. They'd been speaking
louder and louder, their gazes intentionally wandering

11

toward Elizabeth. She was no fool—she knew what they were on about.

Elizabeth sighed and closed her book, trying to ignore the burgeoning dread filling the pit of her stomach. After all, she couldn't exactly concentrate with their antics. She eyed her sisters. "I know what you're doing."

"Whatever do you mean?" Grace asked, batting her lashes innocently.

"Maybe she wants to come to the ball?" Kitty suggested hopefully. She was the youngest of the three sisters, and eager to participate as this was her first season.

"Are you so eager to be married off?" Elizabeth teased.

Kitty's cheeks flushed, setting off the warmth in her brown eyes and brown hair. "I should like to flirt first."

"Kitty," Grace chided even as Elizabeth laughed at their younger sister's cheek.

"Well, you just want to attend so you can see Harold." Kitty drawled out the last word, letting it drip from her lips with a honeyed tone, then she placed the back of her hand on her brow and pretended to swoon.

"Yes, well, Harold means to propose if *someone* would finally set herself on finding someone to marry." Grace looked pointedly at Elizabeth.

It was true, Viscount Scorbridge had been courting Grace for the past year, occupying her entire attention through the season and expressed his intention to do so again this year. There had been comments made when he attended dinner, of his plan to propose when 'the right opportunity presented itself.'

'The right opportunity' being Elizabeth clearing the way for her sister by becoming engaged herself.

Elizabeth brushed off the complaint. "I simply haven't found the right man yet." Her guilt, however, was harder to set aside.

Besides, her statement wasn't a lie. She hadn't found the right man yet. Whomever she married—if she did—would have to love her, the way Darcy loved Elizabeth Bennet or Romeo loved Juliet. She wanted a man who loved her exactly for who she was, who wouldn't roll their eyes or offer a deprecating remark at her clumsiness. Every woman deserved that, and she was no different. And she wanted a man she could love in return, one who made her burn with a fierce passion, who made her crave every second she spent with him. Perhaps even one who handled her direct questions and even read the occasional novel so they might discuss the characters and stories together.

Likely what she wanted would never exist, and so she was perfectly content to be exactly who she was on her own.

Grace crossed her arms over her chest. "You'll never meet anyone if you don't attend balls."

"If I don't attend balls, there will be no one to see me trip," Elizabeth countered.

"You could join us for just this one at least…" Now Kitty was the one trying to feign innocence, her hands clasped behind her back as she twisted side to side, her gaze imploring.

"And you can't say you haven't a thing to wear." Grace put a finger up in the air as if to stop Elizabeth from speaking. "Madame Banner has already delivered every item Mama ordered, and I know for certain she had several ballgowns made especially for you."

Elizabeth was aware. She'd stood stiffly through countless

fittings as velvets and silks were swathed over her body and careful hands pinned and unpinned various styles and embellishments.

Their mother meant to see Elizabeth married this year, if it was the last thing she did. Already Mama was appalled that four seasons had passed without a single proposal for her eldest daughter.

Elizabeth was well aware she had been a disappointment.

Now everyone in her life, including her dearest fellow wallflowers, were insisting she wed.

Anxiety pinched at her chest. "Very well," she conceded. "I'll attend, but don't go lifting your hopes that I'll find some dashing man to sweep me off my feet."

"Yes, you will once you show up in that blue velvet gown with the red silk roses." Grace's wide blue eyes sparkled, most likely already planning Elizabeth's engagement, and then subsequently her own.

Elizabeth offered a tight smile, knowing full well the only one sweeping her off her feet would be herself, as she tripped down the stairs or committed some other graceless folly.

What a night to dread.

JASPER FITZROY, the fifth Earl of Darington, contemplated the underside of the canopy over his bed, his mind ticking through a list of items to see to that day. An abrupt knock came from the door.

Jasper frowned and examined the pocket watch on his nightstand, revealing the hour to be just after nine in the morning. Early for most, but even for him. Then again,

Lord Ranford kept him up into the early hours of the morning, cajoling him into sharing "just one more drink" as he went on and on about a gentleman Jasper didn't even know.

"Forgive me, my lord." The voice on the other side of the door was clearly Jasper's valet, Hughes. "You have a visitor."

"At nine in the morning?" Jasper asked, incredulous.

Wasn't it a bit early for mothers to be forcing their way into his home under feigned excuses to mention their eligible daughters? Whoever named him the most eligible bachelor of the season—again—was decidedly his least favorite person in London. Of all the bloody stupid titles...

"The dowager is here, my lord," Hughes replied.

Jasper frowned. What the devil was his grandmother doing in London?

"I thought she'd retired to the country," Jasper called out from his bed.

"It appears retirement is subjective, my lord."

"Best come in before she hears you." Jasper sat up as the door to his bedchamber opened. "She'll never forgive you if she does."

Hughes entered the room, head lifted with his haughty manner. "She'll always forgive me, my lord."

Jasper snorted. "You're not wrong and you're damn lucky for it."

"Yes, my lord." Hughes set the tray of tea on Jasper's dressing table. "The blue jacket this morning?"

Within the short side of a half hour, Jasper was properly dressed and shaved. Hughes could shave a man faster than anyone and with greater care than a barber who took three times as long.

And considering how much time the estate required of Jasper these days, every second counted.

His grandmother was waiting in the parlor with a steaming cup of tea and an assortment of pastries in front of her.

"Good morning, Bess." He swept toward her, arms open to embrace her.

"You ought to call me Grandmother." She pushed to her feet with the aid of a silver-topped cane and let him wrap his arms gently about her slender frame.

There was a floral fragrance about her, like roses. A sweet scent making him recall when she'd taken him in at her summer estate when he'd been a young teen. After his elder brother, Benjamin, had died and Mother hadn't forgiven Jasper. An ache nipped inside his chest and he pulled away.

"You're not nearly ancient enough to be addressed by anyone as 'Grandmother.'" He popped a pastry in his mouth and almost spat it out. The thing was dry and crumbling in his mouth, sticking in his throat even as he tried to swallow it down with a gulp of scorching tea.

"You smooth-tongued scoundrel." Bess smirked and shook her head. "Haven't changed a bit, have you?"

"Ever steady." He flashed her a grin and poured a bit more tea.

"I see your cook hasn't changed either." She grimaced at the offerings on the pastry tray.

"I haven't time to deal with such things." Jasper considered a jam-filled pastry, wondering if it would be as bad. His stomach growled and he took a risk, biting gingerly. The jam was so tart, his eyes watered and he set the remainder aside.

Bess lowered herself to the sofa and regarded him with a raised brow. "Don't act as if you enjoyed that."

"Oh, it was entirely awful, but better than nothing."

"Is it?" She looked toward the garden, blanketed in snow save for a few scraggly branches jutting out from the sea of white. "You know if you had a wife, she could see to such matters for you."

Jasper lifted his cup of tea and sipped in an effort to stave off the chill in the room, sipping more carefully this time after having scalded his tongue earlier. He hummed in acknowledgment that she'd spoken, though he scarcely agreed.

"Word has it, you've been named the season's most eligible bachelor." Bess smiled proudly at him.

Jasper rolled his eyes. "*Et tu, Brute?*"

"Oh, do go on with your theatrics," she chastised. "This is not the first time. How many times have you been named the most eligible bachelor? Three years? Four? Isn't it about time you use that honor to find a bride?"

"Honor." Jasper scoffed at the word. "And if I'm no longer a bachelor, I cannot continue to hold the title." He set his teacup down. "I'm aiming for a ten-year streak. A decade has a nice ring to it, does it not?"

"It has a horrible ring to it." Bess said with exasperation. "One that reverberates with the sad fact that my life is one without a single great-grandchild."

Ah, this again. Jasper swallowed his impatient sigh more readily than he had the burning tea.

She reached for him. "Jasper, you have an obligation—"

As soon as the word obligation was out of her mouth, she stopped, knowing she'd said the wrong thing.

Heat flared in Jasper's cheeks. He set his teacup down,

minding not to do so with too much force. She hadn't meant that word.

"I'm sorry," she said softly.

He nodded, his shoulders relaxing. And she was sorry. She *knew* what that word meant to him, how deeply it cut into wounds that would never heal.

This obligation never should have been his. Benjamin should have been earl, the way his parents had wanted. Father never thought Jasper was worthy of the role.

"Jasper," Bess said softly. "I'm dying."

His head jerked toward her in shock. In this entire world, she was the only person who cared for him. The only person who had ever bloody well cared *about* him.

His mother had seen him as a playmate for his brother, a guardian. His father saw him simply as the spare heir should anything happen to his oldest son. And Benjamin only ever saw him as a nuisance.

Having Bess retire to the country had been hard enough; to know Jasper might only see her once a year, if that. He'd come to rely on her counsel in years past.

When he'd been a boy, he'd given his love and trust freely and without restraint. Both had been crushed. In the years he'd known her, Bess was the only person he knew he could trust with his thoughts and his heart.

Imagining a life without her was a cold, stark world indeed.

He narrowed his eyes, assessing her appearance for signs of illness.

Her dark eyes were clear and sharp as ever, a healthy flush tinged her cheeks, and she looked as though she'd put on a bit more weight lately, padding her otherwise too-thin frame.

The realization suddenly occurred to him: she was lying.

He turned his head, gazing askance at her. "You are not dying."

She tsked. "Of course I am, I'm old."

"Not so very old."

"Well, nearer to death than I have been to birth in many decades." She sighed and stared at him. "I want to see great-grandchildren before I die, Jasper. Being as you barely attended two events this season—"

"How would you even know that?" He almost grabbed the remainder of the jam tart, but thought better of it. "And the season only started a fortnight ago."

Bess quieted his outburst with a lift of her brow. "I may not live in London, but I have many acquaintances who have remained."

Old biddies who linger on the fringes of ballrooms, critiquing the food and decor while sharing gossip on prospective couples. Old women with nothing but endless stretches of time to meddle.

How very irritating.

Bess clasped her hands over the top of her cane. "If you do not go to balls, you will never find a young lady to wed."

"I haven't even received any recent inv—"

But Bess pulled out an envelope from some hidden pocket in the frilly gray frock she wore. "Oh, would you look at this? An invitation to Lady Gentry's ball tonight!"

"That was from my desk in my office." Irritation prickled up his neck. "I dare say, did Hughes give you that?" Jasper looked behind him where Hughes peered around the doorway and promptly disappeared, a guilty party to be sure.

Bess simply lifted her chin with a benign expression and said, "I do not reveal my sources."

So, definitely Hughes then.

"Please." Bess's face softened. "Please just go and try to find a young woman with whom you might find some semblance of affection."

Jasper resisted the urge to sulk. Bess never asked anything of him. And it was only one ball.

"I won't live forever." She spoke in a feeble voice.

"That's laying it on a bit thick, don't you think?" he muttered.

"I can go thicker." She extended the invitation toward him, her hand trembling as she gave a weak cough.

"Oh, do stop this nonsense." He snatched the invitation from her. "We both know you're immortal."

"I'll be no such thing until I have a great-grandchild." She perked up immediately and beamed a smile in his direction. "And until I see you happily wed to a young woman, I'll be remaining in London."

He nodded distractedly, already dreading the night.

"In fact, I'll be staying here," she added. "To ensure you actually try to find a wife."

He lifted the invitation toward her. "I take it you'll be joining me?"

"Of course. How else could I provide my opinion on who would be a suitable match for you." Her eyes sparkled. "This is going to be such fun."

But Jasper knew that despite having his grandmother close to him once more, the process of her procuring a wife for him would be decidedly *not* fun.

2

*E*lizabeth stood beside the refreshment table at Gentry Place amid a roomful of revelers. Men and women gossiped and flirted all around her while couples twirled in resplendent silks across a glossy dance floor.

Kitty was dancing with a young gentleman who gazed at her like an adoring puppy. One of the many adoring puppies who followed her around that night. And Grace was, of course, with Viscount Scorbridge, their eyes fastened to one another's as if the room full of people had entirely disappeared.

Elizabeth wished *she* could disappear. Certainly that was a better fate than being asked to dance again. She scanned the crowd, glad to see Jillian was being relinquished by an earl her father had insisted she dance with. Likewise, Amy was returning from her set with a man old enough to be her grandsire as she'd been too polite to turn him down.

Another glance about the room confirmed Lucy still hadn't arrived, a mite beyond fashionably late.

The lemonade in Elizabeth's hand had long since gone

tepid, but she still took a sip. More for something to do than out of thirst. The tart sweetness hit her tongue with a cloying note.

"How was the dance?" she asked as Jillian and Amy approached.

"I'd rather not say," Jillian replied stiffly. "So much for my father giving me time to try to find a husband on my own. He still continues to throw men in my direction."

"At least he's not forcing any engagements," Amy offered.

Jillian's shoulder slumped with her sigh. "Yet." She looked back at the man she'd been dancing with as he strutted back to his cohorts. "If he was a bird, what sort do you think he would be?"

It was an odd question, but that was one of the many things that made Jillian so fun to be around. One never knew what might pop out of her mouth. Elizabeth considered the man as he stiffly nodded in greeting to an acquaintance, almost waddling as he passed through the crowd. "Certainly no falcon. Perhaps an owl?"

"I was going to say vulture," Jillian mused, her eyes squinted in thought. "But I could see the resemblance to an owl."

"Come now, don't be unkind." But even as Amy chastised them, she giggled behind her hand.

"Pray tell, what are we laughing at?"

Elizabeth turned toward the woman's voice. "Lucy, we thought you'd never arrive."

"Fashionably late," Lucy said with a sweep of her green silk skirt. "And you'll never believe who I saw when I came in."

"Someone we want to see?" Jillian hedged.

Lucy grinned pointedly at Elizabeth and Elizabeth's

stomach went tight. "Lord Darington. You might want to set your lemonade aside. Remember—?"

"Yes," Elizabeth burst out. "Yes, I remember well enough."

How could she possibly forget the time she'd spilled lemonade all over the poor earl. He'd been polite about the accident, but she'd been so flustered, she mopped up the spill on his cravat, and his jacket, down to breeches where... oh, God...

Fire blazed in her cheeks.

"You touched *it*," Lucy whispered.

Amy and Jillian shared amused looks, even if they were considerate enough not to laugh.

Elizabeth quickly set aside her lemonade, which was whisked away by one of the servants.

"You did say you would allow him to court you," Jillian said.

Elizabeth froze. Had she?

But then she recalled how Hannah, in her wedding bliss, had made them all draw bits of paper to see which of the wallflowers would break her vow and marry next. Elizabeth had drawn the heart, and there had been a discussion about Lord Darington.

Not that a man like him would ever want a thing to do with the likes of her. He was smooth, handsome, and sensual in a way that made her melt when his dark eyes met hers from across the room.

"He is not alone at the ball," Lucy continued.

The heat of Elizabeth's embarrassment quickly chilled. "Isn't he?"

She wanted to ask who he was with, to look around and seek out what beauty hung on his arm.

But doing so would mean confessing how much she thought about him, which admittedly was far more than she ought to. And no one needed to know that but her.

"Who is he with?" Amy asked, flicking a glance at Elizabeth before turning her attention to Lucy.

"His grandmother." Lucy leaned in close. "She stopped me when I came in and told me I was lovely, then asked if I'd met her grandson yet. She was doing it with all the young women. Apparently, Lord Darington is finally intending to find a bride this season to placate her."

"At least women aren't the only ones being forced into marriage," Jillian said derisively.

"Ah, here she is now." No sooner had Lucy announced the news than an older woman with a cane stopped before them. Her back was ramrod straight, her gray hair pulled into an elegant updo, and her eyes were dark and assessing, crinkling at the corners with her smile.

"Hello, Miss Beauchamp, lovely to see you again," the dowager said. "Are these your friends?"

"Indeed," Lucy offered. "Lady Darington, this is Lady Jillian, Miss Honeyfield, and Lady Elizabeth." Lucy swept her hand over to Elizabeth with a flourish, making her stand out among the four of them.

"How lovely to meet you all." Lady Darington cocked her head at the four of them. "My grandson is seeking a wife. Have you met the Earl of Darington yet?"

"Lady Elizabeth has," Amy said unhelpfully.

Lucy nudged Elizabeth forward. "Quite a coincidence when our Elizabeth is next in line to marry."

The dowager's eyes sparked with interest. "I see."

"Your grandson is a kind and charming man who I'm sure

will find a wife befitting him," Elizabeth stammered.

"Well, do ensure you stop by to bid him good evening," Lady Darington said. "I'm sure he would love to dance with such a beautiful young woman."

Elizabeth gave a stiff nod, then curtseyed as the dowager moved on to the next group of women.

"Darington must be mortified to have his grandmother going about like that," Lucy said under her breath.

Jillian played with a dark tendril of her hair. "But it does give you a wonderful opportunity to possibly become better acquainted with him."

Elizabeth shook her head and looked away, refusing to meet Lucy's coy expression. "I don't think so. He wouldn't…"

"Wouldn't what?" Amy asked, her lips turned down in a slight frown.

Elizabeth gave a mirthless chuckle. "Be remotely interested in me."

"Elizabeth, you have so much to recommend you," Amy began.

But Elizabeth didn't want to hear platitudes. Lord Darington was a man with a reputation. He enjoyed beautiful women well and had entertained his fair share.

Elizabeth could be considered lovely with her blue eyes, fair skin, and soft brown hair, but she was no beauty. Certainly, she was no vixen to tempt the likes of Darington.

She didn't want a shallow marriage based on looks and compatible lineage. She wanted a match based on love, on passion.

"You're so kind," Amy began listing Elizabeth's attributes regardless. "Always thinking of others."

Frustration knotted in Elizabeth's chest.

"Please don't," she shook her head. She didn't want to hear how nice she was, how patient, how loyal a friend. Desperate to be free from her friend's words, she took a step back.

Her back hit something solid, which moved away at once, followed by a surprised grunt. She turned in time to see Lady Gentry, the ball's hostess, stagger forward, spilling her lemonade onto the floor and splashing several hemlines. Servants rushed forward at once, armed with damp cloths.

"I...I'm so sorry," Elizabeth stammered out.

Lady Gentry, who was often austere in the best of times, turned a cold gaze on her. "I'm sure it was an accident," the older woman hissed.

Elizabeth nodded tightly and opened her mouth to apologize once more, but the woman was already turning away.

A hand rested on Elizabeth's forearm. She looked up and found Amy at her side. "It wasn't your fault."

Hot tears of humiliation burned in Elizabeth's eyes. Because knocking into Lady Gentry absolutely was her fault. She shook her head. "Forgive me, I need a moment to myself."

Lucy regarded her from behind Amy, brows raised in silent question. Did Elizabeth want company?

Elizabeth shook her head and turned—carefully—from the ballroom, seeking out the retiring room. Several voices were audible from outside the door as she approached.

"And she bumped into Lady Gentry, causing her to spill her drink. Can you believe it?" The statement was punctuated with a cackle of laughter.

Elizabeth skidded to a stop.

"At least there's less competition to snag Lord Darington's attention," the voice continued. "Not that she was competition at all anyway."

More laughter followed the cruel statement.

Elizabeth glanced around, desperate to escape before the women exited the retiring room and discovered her there. Quickly she turned in the opposite direction and headed toward the ballroom once more. Perhaps the patio would be deserted. While the night was tremendously cold, the patio would at least be blissfully empty.

Alone.

That was all she wanted.

She hastened to her destination, eager for silence and the freedom to simply think, to mull over the ridiculous attraction to a man she would never appeal to. That, and relive the horror of what she'd done to poor Lady Gentry. Mama would be horrified when she heard about Lady Gentry. And she would hear about the incident—she always did.

The ribbon holding Elizabeth's stocking up on her right leg loosened.

She froze.

A tickle against her thigh indicated the stocking was still slipping from its tie.

No.

No.

No.

The sound of footsteps sounded around the corner, the familiar cackling laugh of the woman from the retiring room preceding her approach.

Elizabeth walked forward slowly, and her stocking slithered down her leg. The ribbon fell along with it, coiling on the ground at her feet. She snatched it up and ran toward the nearest door, breathing a sigh of relief to find the handle unlocked and the room dark within.

The redolent odor of a cigar and the fragrant notes of leather told her this room was likely the study. She hesitated just inside the door, waiting for her eyes to adjust to the darkness.

Within a second, the stream of moonlight cutting in through the wall-length windows revealed a large desk at the rear of the room, several large leather chairs by the fire, and rows of books on a shelf, all filled with books. She had been correct. She was in the study.

A sigh escaped her then, one that emanated from the depths of her soul. The frustration of everyone insisting that she should marry, her own irritating propensity toward clumsiness that was forever causing Mama to shoot Elizabeth looks veiled with impatience, the hurt caused by the women who had laughed at her in the retiring room, and the enormous relief of finally be alone.

She walked deeper into the room and stayed there a moment, breathing slowly, gathering herself in little shreds of fortitude until she felt ready to return to the ballroom. In truth, she wanted to stay in that dark, empty room all night, to select a book from the shelves and curl up on the leather chair, reading the pages by moonlight.

But she was expected in the ballroom. Already she knew her sisters would be wondering where she'd gone. And Mama as well, of course.

First, Elizabeth knew she must see to her stocking. Modesty nearly had her looking around the room first, which was preposterous when she was obviously alone.

She gathered up her skirt, exposing her leg with the fallen stocking and tugged the errant garment back into place. With her bunched hem pinched against her body by her elbows, she secured the ribbon over the top of her knee and tied it neatly into place.

A glass clinked from somewhere in the shadows.

Elizabeth dropped her skirt, eyes going wide. "Is someone there?"

Even as she spoke into the darkness, her mind scrambled to come up with all manner of excuses for why a glass might clink in the darkness. A glass not settled properly. Or...or...

To her horror, a masculine throat cleared.

All at once, a match was struck and applied to the lantern to her right, bathing the room in golden light and revealing there was indeed a man in the room.

And he was none other than Lord Darington.

JASPER COULDN'T HELP but notice Lady Elizabeth's cheeks were stained red in the soft light, her mouth parted in an 'o' of surprise as she clearly tried to grapple with what to say.

"Forgive me for not making my presence known." He inclined his head.

"You ought to have." Her voice was breathy, lending it a sensual air. "I...my stocking slipped."

Yes, he had seen.

In fact, he truly had been about to announce his presence when he realized she didn't mean to leave immediately after entering the room as he'd expected. He'd admired her a moment too long in the wash of moonlight, her sweet face almost rapturous as she savored exactly what he'd been seeking in coming here: blissful quiet.

And then she'd drawn up her skirts, revealing her slender

leg, her skin flawless and luminescent in the glow of the moon, her ankle neat and her calf shapely. When she'd tied the delicate ribbon around her thigh, he could imagine nothing more than tugging it free with his teeth and letting his lips whisper over the delicate skin of her inner thighs.

His gaze flicked down to her legs, now covered by a heavy velvet skirt.

More's the pity.

"Forgive me," he said again. "I was not expecting…that."

"What are you doing in here?" she asked.

"Relishing a reprieve," he answered smoothly.

And truly he was, from the debutantes whose hungry eyes followed him around the room, from their mothers whose stares were even keener, more predatory, from witnessing how his grandmother went around to each of them in turn, offering them a whiff of his blood to officially begin their hunt.

"In the dark?" Lady Elizabeth frowned slightly, which made her lower lip pout out just so. "Were you hiding?" She pressed. "Or is it…?" Her words tapered off and she bit her plump bottom lip sheepishly.

How he wanted to free that lip with his thumb and press his mouth to hers, to see if she tasted as sweet as he suspected.

He'd always noticed her, the shy woman in the muted pastels who melted into the back of the room, trying to disappear. But a woman like her could never disappear, a woman whose large eyes were blue as the heart of the ocean, whose brown locks suggested they would feel like cool silk running through his fingers. Whose delicate innocence was apparent in every blush, every stammer.

A woman who was too good for the likes of him and he bloody well knew it.

"Or is it what?" He asked, eager for the distraction.

"Or is it that..." Her shoulders lifted in a little shrug, the shadows caressing the lines of her collarbones. "Is it that the darkness is quieter?"

While an odd thing to say, the statement was also entirely accurate. The dark *did* somehow feel quieter.

"Yes, I think you're quite right," he agreed.

"I know." Her outburst almost startled him. "About your promise to your grandmother. There has been talk of little else tonight."

"I wager she approached you and your friends?"

Lady Elizabeth's answer was an apologetic smile, as though acknowledging how humiliating Bess's behavior must have been for him.

"And you wish to throw your hat in the ring?" He asked, his tone intentionally light and flirtatious in the hopes of teasing out another pretty blush.

Instead, her wide blue eyes went wider still. "I would never presume, my lord."

Ah, so that was the way of it. A polite rejection, as he well deserved. And yet he could not help but prod deeper. Perhaps the few glasses of scotch he'd nipped emboldened him, or perhaps her draw was too strong to ignore.

He stepped closer. "Your younger sister is soon to be engaged as I understand it, dependent, of course, on the wedding of her elder sister."

She did not look demurely away as another woman might have, but looked him in the eye as she answered, "You are well informed, my lord."

Desire stirred within him, encouraged by Lady Elizabeth's boldness. He had not had the pleasure of engaging her in much conversation until this moment, and found he was rather enjoying himself.

"It appears I am not the only one in need of an engagement, Lady Elizabeth." The words purred from his throat.

What was he doing goading this innocent? Letting his body ignite with longing for a woman he would never let himself have?

"I should return to the ballroom," she said in reply, "lest I be missed."

As soon as she spoke, the clack of footsteps sounded near the closed door.

"Wait," he cautioned in a low voice.

But she was already walking forward. "I really should—"

Her foot caught at the edge of the Brussels Weave carpet, and she pitched toward Jasper, upsetting an end table. He did not hesitate to reach out, catching her slender waist, keeping her upright as the small table hit the ground with an audible thud.

Elizabeth's eyes locked on his and for the briefest of moments, she did not pull away, indulging him with the soft hint of a sweet, powdery scent. Lilacs, perhaps?

All at once, light exploded into the room as Jasper and Lady Elizabeth turned to find Lady Gentry and several other peers standing stock still in the open doorway, mouths agape.

Jasper hastily dropped his hands from Elizabeth's waist, but not fast enough.

The damage had already been done.

3

———

Elizabeth stared in horror at Lady Gentry accompanied by Lady Whimbly and Lady Hasselton, notably the three most notorious gossips among the ton.

Lady Hasselton lifted her chin triumphantly, the wispy feather in her hair fluttering. "I told you I heard a sound."

"What, pray tell, is happening here?" Lady Gentry demanded, her eyes boring into Elizabeth with what appeared to be blatant disappointment.

"I...I tripped," Elizabeth stammered, her waist still tingling where Lord Darington had caught her, as if the heat of his palms had singed through her dress down to her very skin.

Lady Gentry lifted her brow and shared a skeptical glanced with her friends. "I believe I meant why the two of you are in the darkened study?"

"Oh." Elizabeth swallowed. How was this to be explained away?

"I came in for something a bit stronger than lemonade," Lord Darington answered honestly.

Lady Whimbly smirked. "I see you found it."

And there it was, the implication Elizabeth knew the women had made. That anyone would make.

That a lover's tryst had been interrupted between her and Lord Darington.

Such a thing ruined a young woman. Not only her, but also her family. Her sisters.

Grace.

If Elizabeth was ruined, Scorbridge could never propose to Grace. Elizabeth would be destroying not only her life, but also those of her sisters.

"Perhaps she's trying to trap Lord Darington into marriage?" Lady Hasselton tittered into the wavering fronds of her feather fan.

That's when the idea struck Elizabeth, one borne from a moment of desperation.

"I don't have to trap him into marriage," Elizabeth protested.

Three sets of eyebrows shot up.

Likely four, if Elizabeth had the temerity to look at Lord Darington. Which she did not.

God forgive her for what she was about to do, because Lord Darington likely never would.

Elizabeth squared her shoulders like a soldier preparing to step onto the battlefield. "We are already engaged."

"You?" Lady Whimbly did not bother to mask her incredulity.

A humiliated heat blazed through Elizabeth. She was well aware of how impossible it was that a man like Lord Darington would bother to waste his time with such a bland wallflower as herself.

"The moment was impulsive on my behalf," Lord Darington said from beside her.

Elizabeth snapped her head toward him, desperately trying to keep her expression from reflecting her shock.

"You see, I took Lady Elizabeth into the hall to speak with her." Lord Darington met her gaze, his irises so dark, she could scarcely make out the pupils.

She could get lost in eyes like that, especially when he looked at her as he did now. As if she were the only woman to ever exist in his world.

"I was so overcome with affection that I knew at once I wished to ask her to marry me," he continued.

Elizabeth could not look away, entirely enraptured.

"I could not well say such intimate words in the hall where there might be witnesses and so I pulled her into the study and proposed." He inclined his head in an apologetic manner when one expects immediate forgiveness. "The fault is entirely mine."

"Did you seek her father's permission first?" Lady Whimbly demanded.

Elizabeth's stomach dropped, but Lord Darington simply appeared amused by the question. "Would you be disappointed if I did not?"

Lady Whimbly huffed.

"Well, we must make the announcement." Lady Gentry lifted her head with pride. "Nothing quite makes a ball like an engagement."

She was correct. Every hostess wanted her ball to be on every tongue the day after, and nothing would do that more so than a surprise engagement announcement.

Especially when the impending groom was the bachelor of the season.

"I knew all along, of course." Lady Gentry winked at them, her good humor suggesting she had forgiven Elizabeth for her folly earlier. "When I heard the rumor of Lord Darington needing a bride, I suspected there was a love blossoming between you."

"It's a scandal," Lady Whimbly hissed.

The countess did not believe the story, blatantly seeing the lie.

"It's romantic," Lady Gentry bit out the words and gave her friend a hard look. "And we'll be announcing the engagement at this very moment." She pulled the door open wider in silent demand for Elizabeth and Lord Darington to follow.

Elizabeth tried to swallow, but her throat was suddenly too dry. She stepped forward, prepared for this death march of a walk into the ballroom. Lord Darington matched her step and offered her his arm.

The gesture was gallant and more than she deserved given how she'd trapped him in an engagement.

She slid her icy hand into the warm crook of his elbow where the superfine of his jacket could not hide the strength of his forearm beneath. There was a slight spicy scent to him, something warm and sensual. Beneath that was the smell of spirits about him, indicating precisely what led to his agreement to this preposterous scheme.

Something he would regret later.

How she longed for a moment alone with him, to apologize, to thank him for saving her reputation and that of her sisters. To let him know this was all a façade and she would free him as soon as possible.

But she would not have a moment alone with him, not until after the mortifying announcement of their false engagement and the rounds of surprised felicitations that would follow.

All she had time for before they passed the tall ballroom doors thrown wide open to her fate was a chance to look up at Lord Darington and silently mouth her thanks.

In reply, he simply offered a confident wink, as if to brush aside his noble act.

"Stop the music," Lady Gentry commanded.

When one hosts a ball, they are the god of the night, and the music ceased as soon as the request was issued from Lady Gentry's thin lips.

"I should like everyone's attention, please." She clapped her fingers delicately against her palm, her gloves making no sound at all. "It is my great pleasure to announce…"

Her brown eyes shone with glee as she glanced back at Elizabeth and Lord Darington, pausing for impact and likely to savor the moment her ball would become the most talked-about event of the season.

Every attendee followed Lady Gentry's attention to fix on Elizabeth and Lord Darington.

Elizabeth stomach quivered, threatening to quake through her body and shatter her apart.

She did not want to be here, with so much attention feasting upon her. She did not want to look through the crowd to find the questioning looks of her friends, the shocked confusion of her parents, the enraptured expressions of her sisters, who would love nothing more than to believe such a romantic tale.

No, Elizabeth wished she were anywhere else in all of

England other than Lady Gentry's ballroom on the arm of a man with whom she was presumed to be engaged.

But she couldn't run out now. Not with everyone watching.

Instead, she studied the tips of her velvet slippers peeking out from the hem of her gown and wished that the floor might open up and swallow her whole.

All at once the heat of a hand settled over hers where she held Lord Darington's arm. She looked up to find his hand over hers, a show of encouragement that was echoed in the affectionate expression on his face. He nodded, as if to encourage her to do the same.

Her lips quivered into a smile, and she let herself tip headlong into the darkness of his deep brown eyes.

After letting the dramatic moment hang for far longer than was necessary, Lady Gentry continued, "Lord Darington and Lady Elizabeth Ashbrook are officially engaged."

There was nothing at all official about the betrothal, and yet the oblivious attendees of the ball exploded into applause.

Fear and uncertainty and horror swirled in Elizabeth's stomach, no longer able to deny the truth: she was officially engaged.

And to Lord Darington of all people.

JASPER WAS on his third serving of lemonade, the cloying sweetness mixed with the bite of brandy curdling with the scotch he'd already downed on an empty stomach.

"You finally found one to drag you down, eh, Darington?" An earl Jasper had only been passing acquaintances with until that moment slapped his shoulder as if they were lifelong friends.

What was it about people that made them flock to celebrations? As if the recipient of felicitations might somehow rub off their good fortune onto others.

Jasper set aside his irritation and glanced about. "Speaking of the lady in question, has anyone seen my fiancée?"

"Lost her already, have you?" The earl guffawed in Jasper's face and the irritation flared once more.

Jasper gave the man a playful shove on his shoulder, intentionally setting the earl several inches away to reclaim his personal space. "I had best find her to remind her why she agreed to marry me in the first place."

Several men milling around Jasper cheered, and the earl raised his cup. "Go on then!"

That was all Jasper had wanted to do since they were led out to the ballroom like one of the spectacles on display at Covent Garden. But rather than walking a tightrope with an umbrella or singing in a voice that radiated around the whole theater, Jasper had been publicly announced as engaged to a woman he had seldom interacted with.

A woman appeared in front of him, drawing Jasper to an abrupt halt. The dark-haired woman eyed him critically, her manner aggressive. How peculiar. But then, he knew her to be one of Lady Elizabeth's friends.

"Ah, Miss Beauchamp," he said as her name came to him.

She scowled at him. "If you're looking for your fiancée, she's on the veranda." She stepped forward, hazel eyes flashing. "And if you hurt her, I tell you now, I don't give a fig that you're an earl or would care even if you were a king, I'll kill y—"

"That's enough, Lucy." A blonde woman—Miss Honeyfield —laughed breezily and pulled Miss Beauchamp back with a firm grip. "Don't mind her."

Miss Beauchamp's scowl deepened. "Absolutely he should mind—"

"Go on, go on," Miss Honeyfield intoned in a singsong voice as she waved Jasper on with an overly bright smile.

And while Jasper loved a challenge, he would save putting Miss Beauchamp in her place for another day. Now was for speaking with Lady Elizabeth.

Dear God, his *fiancée*.

What the devil had he done?

He strode toward the doors to the patio with purpose and paused only to cast one last look behind him to seek out his grandmother. Likely Bess would be elated to learn of his engagement, especially after her show of announcing his intention to find a wife to every eligible young woman.

She knew better to point him out to the widows.

Despite Jasper's numerous searches to find Bess, she appeared to be absent.

He pushed through the doors to where the bite of a bitter February wind reminded him winter was still in full force.

Lady Elizabeth stood by the railing in her short-sleeved gown, her gaze lost somewhere in the barren gardens below. A shiver wracked through her slender body, spurring Jasper forward.

He pulled off his jacket as he approached. "Lady Elizabeth, it's far too cold out here to be in a ballgown."

She turned as he placed his jacket over her slim shoulders, her large blue eyes glossy with tears.

"Lord Darington, I'm so sorry."

"You should be, leading a man out here in the middle of winter so he might freeze." He grinned at her to show he was teasing.

But she was not smiling back. "Oh, please don't let me take your jacket." She moved to sweep it from her shoulders, but he stopped her, putting his hands over hers.

"I jest, my lady. I assure you, I am adept at staying warm." He kept his hands on hers. "And as my fiancée, I will always ensure you are warm as well."

Though she was innocent, a sense of innate understanding flashed in her eyes, but she did not smile. "You need not be weighed down long with this engagement." She glanced about, as if confirming they were indeed alone. "We need only maintain the façade long enough for the gossip to fade."

There was a twinge in his chest, a bite of rejection at her words.

Yes, he had gone along with her charade to help her at the time, but now she stood in front of him, draped in his jacket, her rosy lips parting saying she had no interest in marrying him.

His lips twisted wryly. "Gossip can last a week or a lifetime."

"Let us hope this will last only a week."

Disappointment sank its teeth into him. "Lady Gentry wouldn't like that."

Lady Elizabeth sighed, her breath escaping in a puff of frozen air. "You're right, she'll keep the engagement forefront in everyone's mind as long as she can, to ensure we all remember her ball. Although I should hope…"

She looked away shyly, and whatever she meant to say pulled him closer toward her.

Did she hope she might want to know more of him? To take their engagement seriously?

He should not draw such an idea toward him. He knew too well the pain of rejection from those one loved.

And yet…

"Tell me," he insisted.

"My sister wishes to wed Viscount Scorbridge, but he cannot propose."

"Because you have not yet married," Jasper finished.

"As you so astutely pointed out earlier." Lady Elizabeth nodded. "Perhaps we might be engaged long enough for him to at least propose, so my sister can find her happiness."

"And what of your happiness?" Jasper asked.

She blinked. "Is it with you?"

There was no malice to that question, no mockery, and yet any ready answer he might have given stuck fast in his throat.

Was he capable of making someone happy?

He did not often find himself at a loss for words, and the silence between them went heavy.

"The engagement will be over soon," she declared.

"Being my fiancée can't be all that bad." He spoke in jest, and yet there was a weight to his words he didn't want to feel.

She sniffed again, the tip of her nose pink. "Why did you do it?"

The blue of her eyes was almost black in the inky night.

He stared down at her and recalled exactly all the reasons why he'd gone along with her charade.

Because he hated the idea of her in distress. Because there was so much unfairness that one as good and innocent as Lady Elizabeth would be ruined simply by association with him. Because for one brief moment, he hoped he might be good enough for a woman like her.

Instead, he placed a hand over his chest. "Because, my dear, I am a gentleman."

But rather than laugh, she put her hand over his where it still lay over his heart, her gaze still locked on his. "Because you are compassionate, Lord Darington. And I thank you for that."

Jasper had been called many things in his life. Compassionate had never been one of them.

The door opened, letting strings of music and chatter trail out of the golden ballroom as Miss Beauchamp and Miss Honeyfield exited together. "A few more minutes out here and you might cause a second scandal," Miss Beauchamp whispered.

"You can call on her tomorrow," Miss Honeyfield said with an encouraging nod to Jasper before they both slipped back inside.

They weren't wrong. The last thing Jasper wanted was to compromise Lady Elizabeth more than he already had. He put his hand to the small of her back and guided her toward the ballroom.

There was a slick patch of ice of the ground, too large to go around. Jasper carefully led Lady Elizabeth over it. She jerked abruptly, nearly falling. Jasper caught her, steadying her in his arms, nearly losing his own footing in the process.

"I'm such a mess. I'm so sorry," Lady Elizabeth stammered.

"Don't speak of my fiancée in such a way," he chided, and gently released his hold on her to offer his arm.

She put her small hand into the crook of his arm again, bringing with her that sweet powdery fragrance. His nostrils flared slightly as he inhaled the delicate perfume, committing its light scent to his memory.

He liked the way she held onto him, as if he were a rock amid a roiling sea. It made him feel sure and steady; it made him feel needed.

A curl of ribbon slipped from beneath the hem of Lady Elizabeth's gown, the same white satin he recognized from earlier when she'd tied it around her slender thigh.

"Oh, bother." Lady Elizabeth's shoulders sagged. "I should very much just like to return home."

"I'll see to it." He opened the door. "Wait inside. I'll fetch your mother and then have my man ensure your carriage is prepared."

A small smile touched the corners of her lips, and he knew she was grateful for his assistance. There was something to that approval that warmed him from the inside and made him stand a little straighter.

Lady Elizabeth saw him in a different light from any other person he'd ever known. Save perhaps Bess, who, despite their sharp banter, had always thought fondly of him. Jasper found he rather liked seeing himself from the angle that Lady Elizabeth saw him in, even if he knew that angle to be entirely wrong.

4

Elizabeth gazed out the window of the carriage as they rode home, too exhausted to let her empty stare focus on any one thing in the whirling scenery.

"Lord Darington." Mama exhaled his name on a sigh. "Elizabeth, why didn't you tell us he's been keen on you?"

"Too sudden for my peace of mind," Papa muttered. "I don't like it."

"Oh, George, do stop," Mama cajoled. "Our daughter is finally interested in getting married and you're trying to discourage her."

"Darington didn't even bother to ask me first. I'm only the father." Papa folded his arms over his chest with a harumph. "Shouldn't surprise me though, what with his reputation…"

Elizabeth cringed, anticipating a lecture on the kind of man Lord Darington was rumored to be, and the miserable marriage that might make.

"He was carried away with emotion, was he not, Lizzie?" Grace pressed, saving Elizabeth from one of Papa's notorious lectures.

Elizabeth set her forehead against the windowpane, grateful for the cool, hard surface against the thoughts battering around hot inside her skull. "That's what Lord Darington said." She turned to her family and tried to smile.

"Oh, I think it's romantic." Mama clapped her hands. "And at Lady Gentry's ball, no less. She must be so pleased."

Elizabeth turned her face back to the window and swallowed a sigh. Lady Gentry was pleased, all right—so *very* pleased.

"At least she seemed less vexed about you causing her to spill her lemonade," Mama continued.

Elizabeth rolled her gaze back outside toward the flickering scenery rather than look at her mother and unintentionally encourage an upbraiding.

Not that it quelled Mama's words. "Really, Elizabeth, you must always check where you're going when you turn."

"I did look," Elizabeth lied.

"You didn't, I saw you." Mama sighed. "All I ask is that you just try a little harder to be more mindful of where you go and how you step."

"And how I eat," Elizabeth finished.

"Mama," Kitty said with exasperation. "Leave poor Lizzie alone."

A smile touched Elizabeth's lips, grateful for her youngest sister who always acted the part of peacekeeper in the family.

But Mama was not incorrect. So many ridiculous events had lined up to put Elizabeth and Lord Darington in that dark room together, all because of Elizabeth's clumsiness. If she hadn't knocked into Lady Gentry, she never would have left the ballroom. If her stocking hadn't come untied, she wouldn't have wandered into that dark study to fix it. If she hadn't tripped on the carpet and knocked over that table, they might not have been found and forced to explain themselves.

No doubt Lord Darington regretted ducking into that dark room for a drink as much as she did for having gone in there to adjust her stocking. Surely had he been completely sober, he would not have gone along with the engagement.

She tucked her legs together under her skirts, hoping to hide the fact that her stocking was missing, thrown helplessly into her reticule when she couldn't stand the idea of bothering with the dratted thing a second longer.

Her thoughts drifted back to the patio with Lord Darington, when he'd slipped his jacket around her shoulders. She hadn't known she'd been cold until the heavy garment was draped over her. And she hadn't known a man could smell so fine until she breathed in the rich notes of some kind of spice that set a warm pulse thrumming low in her belly.

He'd been so charming, so charismatic. And for all her resolve that she would be confident and in control, she'd slipped on a patch of ice.

And he'd caught her. Again.

"And now your Harold can propose, Grace" Mama interrupted Elizabeth's thoughts and reached across the carriage to grasp Grace's hand.

Elizabeth glanced at her sister, witnessing the beatific smile radiating from her. Grace's apparent joy was a reminder why Elizabeth had done this. She would do anything for her sister's happiness.

Even if it meant being entirely miserable herself.

~

Jasper all but popped out of bed the following morning, knowing Bess was likely already awake and sipping her tea. Presumably reading the gossip rags as she was wont to do.

When he'd requested his carriage to be readied for his departure the previous evening, he'd been informed Bess had already returned to Darington Place. Which meant she was in for a grand surprise this morning.

A glossy curl of ribbon lay next to Jasper's pillow and a smile caught his lips. The very one that had tied the stocking to Lady Elizabeth's elegant leg. He'd thought it lost until he'd gone outside one last time after seeing Lady Elizabeth off, a chance to collect his thoughts before facing Bess, not knowing she was already gone. That's when he'd seen it, the flutter of white among the bare branches of a tree, cradled in the skeleton-like twigs as if being offered to him as a prize.

He curled the silk ribbon around his hand and brought it to his nose, catching the powdery floral fragrance.

Lady Elizabeth's scent.

He immediately recalled flash of her leg, her shapely calf naked, her skin creamy in the moonlight. She'd drawn the stocking up her leg in a way that made him want to follow the path with his fingertips, caressing the silkiness of her skin, up, up, up to the softness of her inner thighs.

Desire stirred within him, coiling as images filled his mind with what he might do, how he might nuzzle the delicate flesh there, eliciting gasps of pleasure as his tongue teased the precious place where her thighs met.

He pushed aside his longing and wound the ribbon into a neat bundle, tucking it into the pocket of his robe. The time had come to ready for the day so he could inform Bess of the good news.

True, he wasn't actually getting married. Lady Elizabeth had made that clear the night before. But at least the engagement would appease Bess for the time being.

His grandmother was at the breakfast table as expected, residing in the spot nearest the window overlooking the garden. Though the plants were dormant and stark, she still enjoyed looking out over the land, noting the various birds that settled close enough to decipher.

"Good morning, Bess." He bent around the scandal sheet in her hands and kissed her soft cheek. "I trust you slept well."

She hummed an agreeable sound.

"Have you read all the news this morning?" He took his seat across from her, grinning in anticipation.

"I have."

Confusion pulled a frown to his face. Surely Lady Gentry's ball would have made all the gossip, even before the engagement. Having it not mentioned would be downright impossible.

"Did you read anything of note?" he pressed.

"In fact, I have." Bess lowered the newspaper to the table, her expression weary. "Your engagement."

He beamed at her and held out his hands as if he might physically catch her approbation in his palms. "Are you not pleased?"

Bess folded her lips against themselves, then sighed again. "I am not."

Jasper's anticipation for her delight gave way to confusion. "Surely you think Lady Elizabeth is a fine enough match for your grandson," he jested.

"I don't know her," Bess replied airily. "And from the conversation I had with her last evening, nor do you." A bird fluttered to the window, something small and brown-feathered. A basic bird by Jasper's standards, and yet it pulled Bess's attention as if heaven sent to frolic about the windowpane simply for her viewing pleasure. She paused to write in her small journal, looking up to note the bird's attributes before setting it aside.

"It's a song thrush," she explained with delight in her eyes. "They sing divinely."

"I do know Lady Elizabeth," Jasper protested, bringing Bess back round to the topic at hand.

And he did, in a way. He knew of Lady Elizabeth, how she had a kind smile for every person who approached her, how she was always surrounded by her friends, and the way her reticence fell away in their presence, how readily her cheeks colored with a pretty blush. He knew despite her perceived shyness, her questions were bold, and that he wished he could see himself the way she viewed him.

Bess huffed another sigh. "You could have at least danced with the girl first. I wanted to see you spinning about on the dance floor, besotted with a young woman. Oh, perhaps the waltz!" She looked up in elation at the thought. "Yes, definitely the waltz."

"You wanted me engaged, and now you have that."

"But I also wanted you to be happy."

"I clearly recall the conversation, you wanted great-grandchildren."

"This is not one of your contracts, Jasper." She settled her hand on the table. "I am your grandmother, not a businessman. And, I must remind you...I am very much dying."

"You are not."

She coughed. A feeble, miserable sound.

Jasper sifted through the newssheet options in front of him.

"Is it so bad I want your happiness too?" Bess asked.

Jasper flipped through the stack one more time before settling on a newssheet detailing investment options for gentlemen. "I am happy."

"Happiness for you is all I've ever wanted." She tsked. "Yes, and great-grandchildren."

"And freedom from the ton so you can retire to the estate in Lancaster," Jasper added.

"Obviously." She settled back into her chair. "Who can deal with these people for longer than a season?" She exhaled a chortle. "Jasper, I want to meet this Lady Elizabeth Ashbrook. I should like you to invite her to dinner later this week."

Anxiety threaded through the cords of muscles along his back. "Of course."

Bess narrowed her eyes, too shrewd for her own good—or Jasper's in this particular case. "You think I won't like her."

"You will adore her," Jasper replied with absolute certainty.

And while he'd intended to avoid seeing his new fiancée, he knew doing so would be impossible, especially now that Bess was involved. There was nothing for it but to prepare for a visit to Langston Place and seeing Lady Elizabeth again.

5

Elizabeth sat before the fireplace in her bedchamber, re-reading the same page over and over without processing the words. She shifted in the seat, turning the cooler side of her body toward the fire. Not that doing so helped her concentrate.

There was no concentrating when thoughts of Lord Darington filled her mind.

Were they truly engaged?

Him to her?

Or had she dreamt it in some blend of nightmare and fantasy all rolled into one?

A knock sounded at her door. "You have a visitor, my lady."

Elizabeth tensed at her maid's announcement. Had Lord Darington come already?

She'd lain in bed far too long that morning, worried that he might arrive and set her heart fluttering like a trapped bird, something loose and wild and unfounded. Then she worried that he might not come, that he'd look back on the events of the previous evening and realize the enormity of his mistake in playing along with this horrible, ridiculous charade.

"It's Lady Brightstone, my lady," the maid said delicately.

Elizabeth's heart became a millstone of disappointment and sank into her belly.

Not Lord Darington then.

Perhaps he truly would not come at all. But surely he would at least seek Papa's permission to marry, for tradition's sake, if nothing else.

Wouldn't he?

"A visit from Hannah is always something to look forward to," Elizabeth said brightly before making her way to the drawing room. And indeed, it was. Usually. When the visit was not in the place of the one person who truly ought to be visiting Elizabeth.

Hannah likely had already heard the news. What on earth would she say?

Several moments later, Elizabeth had her answer as Hannah opened her arms with a squeal of delight as Elizabeth entered the peony-pink drawing room. "Felicitations on your engagement."

Before Elizabeth could caution her friend not to overexert herself, Hannah caught Elizabeth in a hearty embrace, the swell of her pregnancy between them.

"I knew you fancied Darington." Hannah pulled away and clapped her hands excitedly. "Oh, Elizabeth, I'm absolutely overjoyed for you. I so wish I would have been there to see it." Hannah rubbed her belly with great affection and spoke to the mound. "Not that I'm not happy to have you soon, littlest Brightstone." She looked up to Elizabeth once more. "But to see you being announced as engaged at Lady Gentry's ball! She must have been absolutely glowing with excitement."

Elizabeth nodded, unsure where to even begin. After all, she could not lie to one of her dearest friends.

For if one could not be honest to one's friends, who might they ever be honest with?

Hannah's smile fell away and her brow furrowed. "What is it?"

Elizabeth pulled her friend to the sofa and took a breath to begin telling the whole awful tale. "I—"

The butler entered with a slight nod, begging forgiveness as he lowered a silver tray with a thick cream-colored card toward Elizabeth. "Shall I say you're at home?"

Elizabeth's stomach clenched.

Lord Darington?

She lifted the card and read the name in elegant scroll-work. Miss Amy Honeyfield.

The doorbell chimed. The butler looked up with a frown of annoyance.

"Let her in," Elizabeth said. "If that is Lady Jillian or Miss Beauchamp, please show them in as well."

Indeed, the new arrivals were Jillian and Lucy.

Within minutes, the three women had joined Elizabeth and Hannah in the drawing room, a mixture of excitement, skepticism, and confusion evident on all their faces.

"If you're happy, we're happy," Amy said cautiously.

Jillian studied Elizabeth. "Are you happy?"

An unexpected lump fisted in Elizabeth's throat, blocking her from speaking as she readily shook her head.

Lucy's eyes flashed. "What has he done?"

"Protected me from ruin," Elizabeth confessed. "And he protected my family as well. All because of my clumsiness."

The truth spilled from her, every awful detail, from how she'd exposed her leg to him in the study—which made Lucy snort with laughter—to how Lord Darington had played the effusive lover, while recounting the proposal that had never happened in an effort to salvage Elizabeth's reputation—which made Amy sigh wistfully.

"How will you break off the engagement?" Hannah asked, her expression worried.

"I'm not certain." Elizabeth looked down at her hands. "Surely people do not expect us to truly marry. Not with him being who he is."

"He does have a reputation…" Lucy muttered.

Jillian spoke up. "What will you do if he doesn't wish to break off the engagement?"

Elizabeth blinked. Of all the outlandish questions Jillian put forth to the group, this by far took the cake.

A flustered laugh escaped Elizabeth, high-pitched and half strangled. "Of course he will. He was backed into a corner. That is hardly the start of a joyful marriage."

"You never know what might be the start of a joyful marriage." Hannah settled her hands over the mound of her belly and smiled. "Like trying to find a suitor for your friend, only to realize you'd been meant for each other the entire time."

"Your marriage to Lord Brighton is the stuff of novels," Elizabeth protested. "And having read many novels and observed real life, I can assure you that what you have with Lord Brighton is extremely rare. But it's also the marriage I want. Lord Darington is only engaged to me to salvage my reputation for my own clumsy follies. While kind, this is hardly the foundation for a great romance."

Hannah opened her mouth, but before she could speak, the butler appeared in the drawing room once more. "Forgive me, my lady. But you have another visitor."

Elizabeth straightened in spite of herself, for there was only one visitor who might come to call when all her friends were already in attendance.

The butler extended the salver once more with a card at its center, the name printed in a bold font. "A gentleman, my lady."

Elizabeth picked up the card and her heart lurched in her chest. Lord Darington had come to call.

Hannah and Amy shared a look, brows raised in mirror of one another.

"Look at the time," Hannah declared. "I must be getting home to...to have a cup of tea." She grimaced at her poor excuse and offered a helpless shrug.

"I have a painting I must finish before the oils become too dry." Jillian stood and pulled on her gloves.

"And I have a luncheon to prepare for," Amy offered.

They all looked to Lucy who rolled her eyes. "And I have trouble to brew up somewhere."

Jillian nudged her and they all shared a laugh.

"My experience was rare," Hannah said as she passed Elizabeth, and finished in a whisper, "...but an unexpectedly happy union is not impossible." She gave a cheeky grin and left, following the others out the door.

Before Elizabeth could even compose her thoughts, the butler entered once more with Grace in tow as he led Lord Darington into the room. Grace took a seat by the rear window, as far from Elizabeth and Lord Darington as was possible—all the privacy they might have until they wed.

If they were actually going to marry, that is.

Which, of course, they were not.

Lord Darington approached Elizabeth, his dark hair slightly mussed from the vicious wind outside, lending him a wild, dangerous look, especially when paired with his sharp cheekbones and wide, generous mouth. He was taller than most men, making Elizabeth feel at once petite and delicate, as if even his very presence might consume her in the most delicious way.

It was easy to see why women were so drawn to him. That allure of his paired with the extensive wealth of his generous estate and a positive note in Debrett's was precisely why he'd been named the most eligible bachelor for as many seasons as Elizabeth had been out.

"Lady Elizabeth." He took her hand in his, that dark gaze fixing on her as he lifted the back of her knuckles to his mouth.

Her skin burned with the touch of his lips, and she suddenly felt breathless.

"Lord Darington," Elizabeth said on an exhale. "It was good of you to come."

He sat beside her and she leaned in, whispering, "I did not expect you."

It was not entirely a lie. She had not expected him. But she had hoped he might come.

"Of course I would come." He kept his voice low. "I should, after all, ask your father for permission to wed you. I imagine he has taken umbrage by the perceived neglect on my part."

Elizabeth pressed her lips together and Lord Darington

gave a mute chuckle. "As I presumed," he said in understanding.

"I know this…" She indicated the space between them—the situation between them—with her index finger, "has all been rather a mess. I just wanted to apologize again and…"

He caught her hands and held them in the heat of his large palms. "Elizabeth."

Not Lady Elizabeth.

Elizabeth.

Her Christian name.

"And to thank you," she finished in a breathy voice.

"I confess I have somewhat of a favor to ask you." Lord Darington's face was near hers still as they spoke quietly to keep Grace from hearing their conversation.

A quick glance at her sister confirmed her nose was buried in a book, her head respectfully turned away.

"Of course," Elizabeth answered Lord Darington. "Anything."

His brow quirked. "*Anything* opens the door for many more possibilities than I originally had in mind, and even more that warrant consideration."

There was heat in his gaze, as tempting as any flame. He brushed his hand over hers, his fingertips skimming the inside of her wrist just beneath the edge of her lace glove. A liberty no gentleman would ever take with a lady.

But then, if rumors of his reputation were correct, he was not a gentleman.

She pulled in a soft breath and his focus went to her lips.

"What is it you wish, my lord?" she asked, her throat dry.

He considered her for a long, searing moment, then his expression cleared, as though his mind had been made up with a sufficient reply. "I should like to invite you to dinner this week, to meet my grandmother."

Elizabeth fought to keep from squirming and pulled her hands from him. A formal dinner to meet his grandmother?

In a flash of an instant, she thought of all the ways she might blunder such an important introduction. Stumbling into a costly vase resulting in it crashing to the floor in pieces, spilling a rich sauce over the creamy bodice of a new gown, tripping down the stairs and her skirts flying up to reveal parts of her no one should see.

Heavens, there were so many ways this could go wrong.

"I thought she would be delighted at the engagement," Lord Darington mused. "But…"

"She's skeptical," Elizabeth surmised.

He tilted his head in question.

"I understand and will attend." She regretted the words as soon as she'd spoken them, and tried to mask her unease with a nonchalant lift of her shoulder. "Those who care most for us simply want our happiness. Oftentimes a hurried engagement speaks of more troubles than bliss. My father, for example…"

She bit her lip and scrunched her nose.

"So that is what I'm up against, is it?" Lord Darington nodded to himself.

"Indeed."

"Better to know what I'll face going in. Thank you, dearest."

Dearest.

Elizabeth swallowed. "Y…you're welcome, my lord."

He smiled at her, a soft, lopsided grin that stole her heart right from her breast. "Jasper."

Then he kissed her hand once more, rose, and bowed

cordially in her direction, before quitting the room, leaving her hand humming with the memory of his lips and her body hot with a curious sensation she didn't know how to name.

All she knew was that Lord Darington—Jasper—was every bit as much trouble as his reputation suggested. And she had more than the impending dinner to worry about when it came to her faux fiancé.

JASPER FOLLOWED the butler to Lord Langston's study, trying hard not to acknowledge the unaccustomed rattle of nerves.

This was why he'd never met the fathers of the women in his past. Those women had all been widows, young women who had been married off to cadaverous old men, women whose lust for life had yet to be explored and enjoyed. Though his exploits with those women earned him his reputation, he never once debauched an innocent. He'd never set his sights on one for that matter.

Not until Lady Elizabeth.

But he'd kept his distance, not allowing himself to give in to the desire to that draw of attraction that had hooked him the first time he saw her lingering near the wallpaper at a ball over two years ago. The way she'd brightened when her friends joined her, her smile beatific.

The butler announced Jasper to Lord Langston, and Jasper drew a steadying breath, knowing the anxiety knotting his insides would never show on the outside. He'd had a lifetime of experience in hiding his emotions.

After all, showing emotions was like exposing one's jugular to a predator.

No, he'd learned his lesson well.

The butler returned and nodded to Jasper before admitting him inside the study. Dark wood shone beneath a gleam of polish on an array of full bookshelves, and the pipe pinched in the earl's hand curled up with a stream of gray-white smoke, its sweet scent permeating the room.

Lord Langston had the same brown hair as his daughter, though his was sparse above his brow and shot through with streaks of white. He indicated the chair before his desk and drew a puff of tobacco from his pipe.

Jasper sat, feeling much the way he did as a boy at Eton when reprimanded for one infraction or another. "I'm not good enough for your daughter," Jasper announced.

Langston's mouth stretched in an agreeable frown, and he nodded. The smoke released from his mouth as he spoke, "I dare say, this is a good way to start a difficult conversation with something we both clearly agree on."

Some of the tension pinching Jasper's shoulders relaxed. He'd always been good at setting people at ease, even when he himself was not.

"Why are you marrying my daughter?" Langston pinched the bowl of the pipe in his hand and leaned back in his chair. "I'm not normally so blunt, Darington, but this is my daughter. Damn the formalities, I want only her happiness, do you understand?"

The tightness returned in Jasper's shoulders. No matter how much he tried to diffuse the conversation, it would be difficult.

There was no empathy in Langston's narrowed eyes. "You don't require her dowry as far as I'm aware. Your reputation has drawn you to more worldly women. You've never shown an inclination toward marriage. And what's more, you've never displayed a modicum of interest in my Elizabeth." He leaned forward in his seat, the leather creaking beneath his solid frame. "You never even approached me to court her, let alone pay your addresses."

Before Jasper could offer any reply to the very astute accusations laid at his feet, Langston went on, "Have you compromised my daughter, sir?"

"I have not." Jasper's voice was firm, wanting to leave no question in Elizabeth's father's mind as to her innocence.

Jasper was a rake—or, at least, he had been once upon a time—but he had never been *that* kind of rake.

Langston regarded him for a moment, as if weighing his words, a father wanting desperately to know his daughter was a good girl.

A bolt of rage flashed through Jasper, surprising him with the intensity of the need to defend her. "Do you think so little of your daughter that you would question her character?"

Langston blinked in surprise.

"You know she is not that kind of woman," Jasper bit out. "No matter the kind of man you think me to be, you know your daughter."

Langston nodded, having the good grace to at least appeared shamefaced. "The expediency of the engagement had left me afeared..."

"Pressure."

"I beg your pardon?"

"We have both felt the pressure of our families to marry," Jasper replied easily. "Viscount Scorbridge cannot propose to Lady Elizabeth's sister until she is set for marriage herself. And my own grandmother has insisted I find a bride. No sooner had I made the promise to find a woman to marry than the gossip spread like fire. I could scarce move at Lady Gentry's ball for the debutantes and their mamas. Truly, why all women are not hunters, I do not understand. They would put us men to shame with their innate ability to stalk even the most elusive prey."

Langston snorted a humorless laugh. "Ah, yes, because you are the bachelor of the season."

Jasper grimaced, hating the pomp of how ridiculous the title sounded in such a tense setting.

"So, you proposed to my daughter to avoid having to deal with debutantes and their mothers," Langston surmised.

"I knew the woman I wanted," Jasper replied in all earnestness. Because he *had* always wanted Lady Elizabeth.

Even if he knew he would never allow himself to have her.

"You are correct." Langston drew on his pipe and settled a hard look at Jasper. "You aren't good enough for my daughter. But I believe your intentions are pure."

A knot of guilt squeezed in Jasper's gut.

"Therefore, I will give you my permission to wed her." Langston nodded. "Not that you have given me much choice. I'll not ruin her by refusing you."

"Thank you, sir." Jasper forced a smile to his lips and wished that he was an innocently besotted suitor who had come to ask for Lady Elizabeth's hand in marriage. That he was a different person, and this entire situation could be in earnest.

He pushed to standing and approached the door.

"And Darington?"

Jasper paused and turned back to Langston.

Smoke coiled up from the pipe, adding a particularly

vicious note of malice to the earl's voice. "If you hurt her, I will call you out."

That marked the second threat on Jasper's life he had received in as many days.

Still, those threats were nothing compared to the pressure he put on himself. For even though this engagement was not to last, Jasper was determined not to hurt Lady Elizabeth.

Even if it meant casting the expense upon himself.

6

The scenery flew by faster than usual as the carriage made its way to Darington Place.

"Do stop fidgeting, Elizabeth," Mama admonished.

Elizabeth froze even as ants of anxiety continued to wriggle under her skin. "Why did you make me wear white?" A quiver sounded in her voice, a reminder of how barely composed she was.

The day of the dinner arrived far too quickly for Elizabeth's liking.

Much like the carriage.

Truly, why was it going *so* fast?

"White is a becoming color on you." Mama turned to glance over Elizabeth and smiled in approval.

"Until sauce is splashed on my skirt."

"Then don't spill." Mama sighed. "Truly, Elizabeth, just be more mindful."

Elizabeth gave way to the energy zinging around inside her and shifted in her seat.

Mama never understood that Elizabeth didn't mean to be

messy or clumsy. No matter how hard she tried, there was always something that fell on her, or rendered her path uneven.

"Ah, here is Darington Place now." Mama smiled as the carriage rolled to a stop.

Elizabeth clung to the seat, wishing she could remain there in the warm quiet of the coach. Alone.

Preferably with a good novel.

But the door was whisked open by a footman, letting the chill sweep in along with the stark understanding that she was out of time.

Mama exited the carriage first with Elizabeth following suit. They were greeted by the butler and led into a vast foyer, far grander than the one in their townhouse. Mama's brows lifted toward Elizabeth in the ultimate maternal approval, and Elizabeth could practically hear her mother's words in her mind.

An enormously wealthy man—well done, Elizabeth.

They were led to the parlor where Lord Darington—Jasper—waited with his grandmother.

Jasper immediately went to Elizabeth's side, first addressing her mother. "Good evening, Lady Langston." He smiled at Elizabeth. "Welcome to my home, darling."

Darling.

There was a tug in Elizabeth's chest at the endearment. Did he have to address her as such?

"Your home is lovely," Mama said, the compliment one of truth as much as politeness.

"His mother did an exquisite job with her decorating." Lady Darington shot Jasper a look. "He's done nothing with it since. Evidently, he's been waiting on a wife to take on the task for him." At that, his grandmother turned to Elizabeth.

She froze. Was this a test of some sort?

"Grandmother, you already know Lady Langston," Jasper said.

The two older women nodded at one another.

"And this is Lady Elizabeth." Jasper grinned. "My fiancée." He held Elizabeth's gaze, as if he was proud of her. As if he wanted her there. "And Lady Elizabeth, this is my grandmother, the Dowager Countess of Darington."

"What a delight to meet you again, Lady Elizabeth. You appear to be the woman who has captured my grandson's heart." Lady Darington lifted her chin, her eyes narrowed in assessment.

Elizabeth was saved from having to reply by the fortunate ring of the dinner bell.

Jasper offered his grandmother his arm and led the way to the dining room where the table had been set as if an entire party of attendees was expected. Brilliant red roses formed a centerpiece on the table, with a rose at each place setting, the stem scraped free of thorns.

They slid into their seats as servants rushed forward to lay their napkins in their laps. Elizabeth pulled off her gloves.

A smudge of black showed at the wrist. When had she even been near something dark to stain the white kid leather?

Perhaps when she'd held onto the seat, wishing to remain exactly where she was.

"You are a pretty thing," Lady Darington said abruptly.

Elizabeth's cheeks burned under the dowager's curt praise, not entirely liking the way the compliment was phrased. A *thing*. As if she were a bauble to take out and put on and then return to its box.

Still, she mustered a smile. "Thank you."

"Do you have sons?" Lady Darington asked Mama almost before Elizabeth had finished speaking. "Forgive me, I don't recall. My memory isn't what it once was."

The servants approached with tureens and ladled soup into their bowls.

White soup.

A wave of relief washed over Elizabeth. At least if any did splash on the delicate white silk, it would not be glaringly evident.

Mama cleared her throat. "Daughters. I have three daughters, but my mother had a bevy of sons."

Elizabeth looked at her soup and focused on eating the meal without spilling as her mother had suggested in the carriage. The task was preferred to listening to the conversation at hand with her mother trying to convince the dowager that Elizabeth might yet bear sons someday.

"After this, we ought to discuss our stores of livestock," Jasper said. "Or perhaps if you find her hips suitable for birthing."

Elizabeth looked up in time to see Lady Darington's face go red with shock. "Jasper."

"She is to be my wife, not a broodmare, Grandmother. Please be respectful."

Lady Darington smirked at the reproach. But still, she nodded graciously to Elizabeth. "Forgive me, I've apparently been too long in the country."

"She understands the need for an heir," Mama answered hastily.

And while the answer felt as inappropriate as Lady Darington's inference to needing a son, Elizabeth was grateful to be saved from speaking.

"Have you considered a date yet for the wedding?" Lady Darington asked before taking a small sip of the soup.

Elizabeth wanted to shrink inside herself. If they set a date, then they would have to begin planning. And once planning was underway and money had been spent and people employed...well, calling off the wedding would be more difficult.

"Possibly spring," Jasper answered at the same time Elizabeth said, "Next fall."

Lady Darington frowned, and sweat prickled at Elizabeth's palms. She picked up her spoon to eat her soup, but her fingers trembled and the handle slipped from her hand, clattering noisily back into her bowl.

Three sets of eyes looked pointedly at her and heat colored her cheeks.

"Forgive me, it slipped," Elizabeth whispered, utterly mortified.

"I never did like these spoons," Jasper mused. "There's no real grip to them."

Elizabeth gave him a grateful smile.

Lady Darington looked between them. "So, spring, then?"

Once more Mama jumped into the conversation. "Spring truly is such a lovely time to wed. I think it's perfect."

Elizabeth opened her mouth to protest, but Mama kept speaking. "I'm thinking April."

April was only two months away.

Elizabeth stiffened. "I don't..."

"You're absolutely right, Lady Langston." Lady Darington

leaned back slightly as a servant cleared away the soup bowls. "That will give them the remainder of the season to acquire anything they need for their home while in London. And perhaps a honeymoon in Italy."

A honeymoon?

Elizabeth's heartbeat thundered in her ears.

This was all happening far too fast.

"I think…" Elizabeth interjected.

"Oh, Italy would be perfect for spring, before it becomes too hot there," Mama gushed. "And I was thinking hyacinths for the flower arrangements. They're such a lovely spring flower, do you not agree?"

Except that Elizabeth did not care for hyacinths, their scent far too earthy for her liking.

"Will you simply be planning the entire wedding for us, or do we have a say?" Jasper interrupted and Elizabeth relaxed somewhat, grateful he had spoken up.

The older women ceased speaking for a breath of a moment as they looked at him, then returned their focus to one another once more.

"Absolutely hyacinths," Lady Darington agreed as the servants entered and the briny, savory scent of herbed meat filled the air.

Elizabeth took a slice of beef, noting the distinctly reddish-brown sauce that posed a terrible threat to her pristine gown. The knot of anxiety in her stomach tightened.

"I should think Elizabeth would like to offer input on the wedding," Jasper said.

Mama turned to Elizabeth, her expression bland. But Elizabeth knew everything that banal look hid. Doubt that Elizabeth would truly have a care regarding what happened at her own wedding. Disappointment that Elizabeth had never been that daughter she'd always wanted.

Grace had been that child with Kitty quick at her heels. Both filled with squeals of adoration for fashion and gossip. Both graceful and elegant.

Whereas Elizabeth much preferred the company of a book to any companion at a social event.

But what would Elizabeth actually like for a wedding?

She considered the possibility as the servant completed his way around the table to deposit a slice of beef and accompanying sauce onto each plate.

"I should like a wedding in the country, I think," Elizabeth answered earnestly. "In a small parish church with only our family present. And in the summer, so we can use wildflowers."

The image came to mind of a spray of daisies flecked with brilliant irises adorning the pews of a chapel, sunlight streaming in through a window of stained glass. And Jasper at the end of the aisle, waiting for her in a fine suit, that lopsided grin on his face.

Her breath caught.

Where had that last bit come from?

Letting her imagination dip into the possibility of their marriage was far too dangerous, something surely to be avoided.

She quickly cut a piece of beef and lifted it to her mouth, so she did not have to speak further, dream further.

Want what was not meant to be.

But as she brought the bite to her lips, the square of beef slipped off the tines and tumbled to her bodice where it rolled like an acrobat down the front of her dress. Brownish-red juice trailed down the creamy silk in a stain that would likely never come out.

The table went silent, and Elizabeth did not need to look up to know everyone stared at her.

She had single-handedly ruined the dinner. And presumably any chance that Lady Darington might actually approve of her.

WITHOUT THINKING, Jasper dredged a forkful of beef in the largest pool of juice on his plate, lifted it to his mouth and let it intentionally fall.

The fork clunked to the floor, but not before the damage was done. A splotch of brown-red stained the smooth, clean lines of his white cravat and the meat fell into his crotch, leaving a brownish-red stain that soaked into his napkin.

Suddenly the stares that had fixed on Elizabeth were now pinned on him.

He shrugged a shoulder. "As I said, there is no grip to the silver."

A servant rushed forward to collect the fallen fork as another presented him with a fresh one.

Bess stared at Jasper, first in horror, then confusion. Then her gaze cleared as understanding dawned, and her expression softened. She turned her attention back to Elizabeth once more. "Tell me, Lady Elizabeth, what do you enjoy doing with your time?"

The question was asked in a softer tone than her previous queries, which had been flung Elizabeth's way as if they were an assault. As though she had already deemed Elizabeth to be merely be after Jasper's wealth.

The softness in her demeanor continued as Elizabeth discussed her love of reading, a pastime she and Bess shared, as well as interest in music, with a shy admission of a dislike of needlepoint, which made Lady Langston go red in the face, but widened Bess's smile.

Oddly, despite the stained clothing and dropped utensils, dinner was a success.

Jasper took Elizabeth's arm leading her toward the door afterward while Bess and Lady Langston hovered in the back, nattering on about wedding details.

"Your poor valet, having to lift that stain from your cravat." Elizabeth's eyes lowered to the bit of white at his throat.

"At least he was spared from also having to contend with my breeches, thanks to the sacrifice of my napkin."

Elizabeth bit her lip. "My maid can likely provide some tips. I'm afraid she's had to become rather adept over the years, dealing with the likes of me."

"My valet is more than capable," Jasper replied, feeling as though he needed to defend Hughes. And yet the idea of having a reason to appeal to Elizabeth's counsel was too appealing to decline entirely. "But I shall keep your offer in mind should he have need."

"I know why you did it."

Jasper lifted his brow. "Propose to you?"

"Why you spilled your food on yourself." Her brow furrowed. "Intentionally." That pretty blush he was finding himself so fond of colored over her cheeks. "To keep the attention off me. Because of how clumsy I am."

"A couple should always be a matching pair, or so I think." He plucked at his cravat and winked.

"You don't have to do that..." Her lips twisted in thought. "Protect me."

Jasper almost frowned. *Had* he been trying to protect her?

In fact, he really hadn't bothered to consider why he done it. There had been a moment of shock as that lucky piece of meat bounced off her bosom and trailed down the front of her gown. He didn't have to look at his grandmother and her mother to know they stared at her in barely concealed horror. He'd seen the humiliation reflected on Elizabeth's pretty face.

And then he'd just done it. To spare her from mortification. To keep them from regarding her with any level of scorn.

Yes, damn it, to protect her.

The realization hit him like a physical blow.

He'd learned a long time ago he was bad at protecting people. Enough that he swore to never do it again.

And now here he was, with a stained cravat and a hero complex, when he knew bloody well he was the villain.

His thoughts drifted to that fateful day, when he'd been so tired of playing protector. When he'd shucked off his clothes and plunged into the idyllic lake at Fitzroy Manor that summer, the icy water sluicing across his skin, barely touching the fire of his rage at the unfairness of always being weighed down by his brother.

"I've lived with myself long enough," Elizabeth continued, pulling him back from a place he did not wish to go. "I know well how to handle my foibles and suffer through my mistakes. I haven't perished from embarrassment yet." She offered a brave smile. "So, you see, I really have no need of saving. Your wardrobe should be quite pleased. After all this isn't the first time your clothing has suffered because of me—"

Her words cut off, and suddenly Jasper was hit with a different memory—this one far more pleasant. Another ball at Lady Gentry's, though the season before, when Elizabeth had mistakenly spilled her lemonade all over him.

He glanced over his shoulder to find Bess and Lady Langston were still chatting by the study. She waved Elizabeth's mother inside, leaving Jasper and Elizabeth momentarily alone.

"You mean the spiked lemonade?" Jasper asked in a velvety voice.

His teasing was rewarded with stains of color on her cheeks.

"Lucy was the one who put the brandy into the lemonade," Elizabeth protested. "It was hers."

Jasper leaned an arm against the wall, bracing his weight on one side of her, but left the other side open should she wish the space away from him. She did not move, but instead gazed up at him with blue eyes, transfixed as if waiting for him to share the story of how she had whisked her handkerchief and hastily dabbed at his waistcoat, following the trail of liquid until she realized she was brushing her fingers over his groin.

"It was your handkerchief," he purred.

Her mouth parted in a gasp, that full lower lip tempting him beyond reason. He could imagine sucking it gently between his lips, letting his tongue graze across that delightful plumpness. Would she gasp as she'd done just now? Moan? Melt against him so his hands could stroke over her body?

"Are you going to kiss me?" She whispered the question so

softly, he could never have heard it were he not so close to her.

"Do you want me to?" He studied her expression, relaxed and ready to yield to him.

The answer was echoed in her eyes, bright with an undeniable interest, her slender throat squeezing as she swallowed, little pink tongue darting out to moisten her lips.

God, how he wanted to kiss her. To sample the lushness of her mouth, to bury himself in her beauty, her sweetness.

But she was not meant for him.

The engagement would soon be called off and her innocence would need to remain fully intact.

He would not put her at risk of true ruin.

Damn it, this was why he'd only dallied with widows in the past.

"And that's how we ended up with such a monstrosity," Bess's voice sounded down the hall, followed by a laugh with a volume deliberately meant for him to hear.

Jasper leaned back from Elizabeth. The lightheaded passion she elicited in him did not abate, even when freed from the draw of her proximity.

Elizabeth scarcely spoke as Lady Langston thanked them profusely for their hospitality at dinner.

"I look forward to seeing you tomorrow," Lady Langston said as she pulled on her gloves.

"More wedding planning?" Jasper asked dryly.

Bess sniffed. "We need an engagement party first."

Elizabeth's face paled somewhat. "I beg your pardon?"

"Do you really think I'd allow my eldest daughter to be engaged and not throw a party to celebrate?" Lady Langston clasped her hands in front of her.

"And I only have this one grandchild." Bess meant the reminder to be endearing, but it nudged against his heart like a burr.

After all, it was his fault he was her only grandchild.

Elizabeth gave Jasper a desperate look, but who was he to stop a proud mother and meddling grandmother?

With one last silent, helpless entreaty from Elizabeth, she and her mother swept out into the chilly February wind and to their waiting carriage.

No sooner had their front door closed, than Bess turned to Jasper. "Well," she sighed.

Jasper waved his hand, expecting Bess's critique of why he ought to have a proper go at a woman he'd known longer, and whatever else the impending miserable conversation entailed. "Let's have it."

"I dare say dinner was a success, though I don't know that our laundress will agree." Bess looked pointedly at his stained cravat, but even as she did so, a smile blossomed on her lips. "And I commend myself for having a discussion with your chef to do better or find himself a new employer."

"The meal was surprisingly delicious," he conceded.

"I could not stand by a moment longer while that man failed at his job." Bess put her hands on her hips. "Mind you stay on him when I leave."

"And what of Lady Elizabeth?" Jasper asked, unable to stop himself.

"Lady Elizabeth is a delight," she effused, as delighted now as she had been irate only a moment before. "An absolute delight." Her lashes lowered as she considered the gravy stain on Jasper's cravat once more. "But you already know that." A smile split Bess's face. "I can see why you love her."

Love.

Jasper almost blanched. Because love was what engaged couples should feel for one another, yet aside from Bess, there hadn't been anyone in this world he loved. No one he intended to soften his heart enough to let in.

Bess narrowed her eyes, her expression going shrewd in that way it did when she saw more than he'd like her to. "Don't ballock this up, Jasper."

"Bess, I…" he hesitated.

"What is it, my boy?" She put her free hand on his forearm, concern in her dark gaze.

"She's too good for me," Jasper said simply.

At that, Bess gave a laugh. "Oh, well, if that's all." She patted his back. "Any woman would be lucky to call you their husband. Put any of those fears from your mind."

Jasper nodded, pretending to be reassured, when in fact he was anything but. Those fears would never leave his mind. Especially with a woman like Elizabeth.

7

The following morning, it was not merely Lady Darington who waited for Elizabeth and her mother in the drawing room, but also Jasper.

Elizabeth drew up when she saw him, her heart pounding.

She had scarcely slept the night before for thoughts of him, the way he had gazed down at her, how he had studied her mouth. As if he meant to kiss her.

Stupid little fool that she was, she had wished that might happen.

Of course, it didn't. And it wouldn't. Not when they were not truly engaged. Not when all of this was simply a façade.

But the way he'd looked at her then with that lopsided smile on his face made every rational thought in her head melt into a pool of hope.

"I say we make it the event of the season," Lady Darington declared.

Elizabeth tensed. "I beg your pardon?"

The event of the season would mean a considerable number of guests. And she would be the sole focus alongside

Jasper. Everyone would notice each wobble, every stumble, as well as any possible small stain or rip. "How many attendees did you have in mind?"

Lady Darington folded her gloves in her lap as she took a seat, completely oblivious to Elizabeth's distress. "I want to have at least one hundred people there. Perhaps more." She beamed at Jasper. "My grandson is getting married, and I want the world to know."

Mama clapped her hands together, her eyes sparkling. "This will be such a delight!"

But Elizabeth did not feel delight. She felt dread, the icy darkness of it twisting her gut and leaving her stomach roiling. And while she was perfectly capable of speaking up to protest the idea of such a publicized affair, she could not bring herself to dim the joy on the faces of her mother and Jasper's grandmother.

A hand touched her arm, pulling her attention to where Jasper stood at her side. "May I speak with you in private? And by private, I mean a quiet corner of the room." He nodded toward the rear window where Grace had read her book when he came to call on Elizabeth after the announcement of their engagement.

She nodded and followed him to the corner. Both Mama and Lady Darington paused in their chatter for a moment to watch them walk toward that back corner and shared a smile that seemed to say "ah, young love."

"You don't appear overjoyed," he said in a low voice.

"They'll hear you." Elizabeth shot a glance back to where Mama and Lady Darington had their heads together, both talking excitedly.

Jasper scoffed. "They won't. Look at them."

Elizabeth glanced over as both women laughed in shared joy, and Mama gave a merry little clap of her hands again.

"They're so happy." Elizabeth smiled to watch them, these women reveling in what they had wanted for so long.

They would be heartbroken when the engagement came to an end.

Jasper took in Elizabeth's downcast expression. "I know you do not want the event of the season for our engagement party. Likely you do not even want the party at all."

"There is no real engagement to celebrate," she whispered. "But no, I do not want a party at all."

"Then all you need do is say as much." Jasper turned toward the women, opening his mouth to speak, but Elizabeth stopped him by grasping his hand. Neither of them wore gloves and the warmth of their naked fingers touching was like a jolt through her.

As if hit with the same sensation, Jasper looked down at where she still held his hand in hers.

"Let them have this," Elizabeth said.

"But you don't want a large party." Jasper shook his head. "You should not have to endure something you do not want. It is, after all, our engagement and not theirs."

"They won't have a wedding," Elizabeth said softly. "Let them have this."

The expression on Jasper's face softened from concern to consideration. "I'll be by your side the whole night."

Elizabeth gave a humorless laugh. "For every trip and spill?"

"I'll catch you if you fall and we'll insist on only foods that will not stain."

"I do not think such a thing exists." But even as she spoke, a smile touched her lips.

He grinned back in a way that warmed her heart more than it should. "Then we will match once more if you do spill something."

"I told you last night, you don't need to protect me." The last thing she wanted was Jasper being burdened with responsibility for her actions. She could not even mind her own actions, let alone knowing she was dragging someone else down with her.

"I assure you, we will be the happiest couple." Jasper gazed down at her as if he could not stop keep his eyes off her.

And though she wanted to lose herself in those fathomless dark eyes, she understood his actions for what they were—a façade.

She had not realized what an actor he was until that moment. Suddenly, it all made sense. The way he called her *dearest* and *darling,* the way he looked at her like she was the only person to ever exist in the world, even how he had studied her mouth as if he meant to kiss her.

None of it held any true meaning. He was simply playing the role she had forced him into. And she would do well to remember that.

"I imagine it is difficult of you to take time out of your day to attend the engagement party planning," Elizabeth said. "At least we will not see one another until our engagement party."

The statement was meant to be one of consolation. What man wished to burden his schedule with a woman he did not mean to marry?

But his jaw seemed to go tight under his grand smile. "Indeed." Then he offered her his arm and led her toward the sofa where tea had been set out and the engagement party planning was already underway.

～

JASPER SAT at Elizabeth's side as Bess and Lady Langston discussed the courses of a grand feast, the hothouse flower arrangements, and argued over which orchestra would be the perfect fit for such an event.

In the end, Bess won, and Lady Langston learned Jasper's grandmother was a true force to be reckoned with. Bess was not one to lose. Ever.

Through it all, Elizabeth remained agreeable. Yes, purple hyacinths and white orchids would be lovely. Yes, the fish course would be a nice addition. Yes, the order of the songs was perfect.

But Jasper knew she wanted none of it, that she merely went along to please her mother and Bess.

There was a great kindness to Elizabeth. She was truly a good person, wanting only to bring joy to others.

Which made him only want to protect her even more.

Perhaps after so many years, that need to shelter someone weaker than himself was inherent. If the engagement party was to continue, he would ensure he did remain at her side, to shield her from any wayward comments, and keep her solidly on her feet.

In truth, he had been looking forward to seeing her before their engagement party, to get to know the woman who appeared so shy from a distance, but up close was bold and open with her assessments. But her claiming they need not waste time on one another until the engagement party was a stark reminder that this was all just for show. A play with an end.

But in that moment, as she nodded in a sweet, agreeable nature to an event she wanted no part of, he wanted to be the kind of man who deserved to be engaged to her. Even if it all was an act.

But whatever his good intentions had been, they were dashed the next morning with the delivery of the scandal sheets.

Bess gave a chagrined sigh as Jasper sat down to breakfast the following morning. "I understand your haste."

"And here I thought I was late to breakfast," he jested.

"I'm referring to Lady Elizabeth." She settled the paper in front of him.

There, in black-and-white print, was the story of how just moments before the engagement that stunned London society, Jasper had been found in the study alone with Elizabeth. Already a scandalous thing, but especially when paired with his notorious reputation.

The article went on to justify their placement in the study for his wanting privacy to propose, but the damage was likely already done.

"It's a good thing you love her," Bess said. "Or that girl's reputation would be in shreds."

Jasper set the paper down. "Especially with my reputation," he muttered.

Bess flicked the scandal sheet away as if it were a bug. "You haven't been that man for years. Don't let your past define you."

"Despite your encouraging words, the ton has already seen

to that. And now my folly as a youth might put Elizabeth at risk."

Bess patted his hand. "Don't be silly, Jasper. Once you wed her, any question of her reputation will be laid to rest."

Jasper nodded.

"You do love her, don't you?" Bess asked.

"I'm engaged to her."

Bess lifted a brow. "That isn't an answer and you well know it."

"Of course." Jasper gave her an easy smile. Because he did know very well he hadn't given her an answer and therefore was not lying.

A bird landed on the window ledge, its feathers iridescent in the glint of sunlight, and Bess sucked in a breath, hastily grabbing for her little notebook.

Jasper accepted the reprieve from the conversation and enjoyed a pastry, one that actually melted in his mouth as he ate it. The cook really had taken advantage of Jasper's busy schedule. He would do as Bess suggested and stay on him to continue his efforts after she eventually returned to the country. Which might not be for a while if she remained until the engagement was broken.

But even with the idea of breaking the engagement, Jasper and Elizabeth first had to make the ton believe they truly did love one another. That Elizabeth had not been a woman Jasper had merely seduced as a conquest.

Not that he'd ever been that man, but the ton made of a bad reputation what they liked.

And if he did not play his cards right with this, they would do the same to Elizabeth.

8

*E*lizabeth arrived downstairs to a bouquet of hothouse lilacs and her father's scowling face.

"I wish I'd known about Darington's proposal," Papa said. "I might have declined his offer for your hand in marriage." He huffed an angry growl.

He shoved the newssheet toward her and nausea rolled through her as she read the sordid details of how she and Jasper had been found together in the semi-dark study. Everyone would be speaking of this for weeks.

She put a hand out to steady herself. How were they to fix this?

Papa indicated a full bouquet of lilacs. "He sent these for you with a note that he would come to collect you at quarter past four this afternoon for a ride through Hyde Park."

"You read her note?" Grace asked, horrified.

"This is my house," Papa said, red-faced with an unaccustomed show of anger. "I'll read any missive any of my daughters receive from any gentleman I feel the need to call into question."

But Elizabeth was not vexed by his invasion of her privacy. Second to her gnawing malcontent at the ton being privy to her and Jasper being in the study alone, she was also concerned with the idea of Jasper coming by to take her on a carriage ride through Hyde Park. That would be during the fashionable hour, when people were out to be seen. She and Jasper would be alone together, in an open carriage, of course, so people would know the outing was innocent. But he would be acting again with those charming smiles, doting endearments, and deep gazes that threatened to steal her heart.

"The fashionable hour in Hyde Park," Kitty exclaimed, her eyes alight with the excitement of a young woman enamored by everything in her first season. For her, society was a secret world of glittering balls and stunning gowns and romance waiting to sweep her off her feet. "What will you wear?"

Before Elizabeth could worry that she hadn't a single stylish thing to wear for the fashionable hour, Grace sat up straight. "I have just thing for you."

By the time Jasper arrived at quarter after four, Elizabeth was cinched into a peony-pink velvet jacket and skirt over a cream-colored bodice with a matching hat. Though Elizabeth had always protested such fripperies, she could not deny that in such a fine gown, she felt beautiful.

Even more so when Jasper's eyes widened at her appearance and a slow, appreciative grin showed on his handsome face. "You look lovely."

She nodded her thanks and allowed him to lead her to the open carriage.

Perhaps she ought to let her mother talk her into such gowns at her next fitting, or have Grace and Kitty join her at the modiste.

The day was warm, thanks to the sun high overhead tempering the icy wind sweeping off the Serpentine. Still, the chill nipped at their faces and left Jasper's nose and cheeks red.

"I know you did not intend to see me until the engagement party," Jasper said when they'd rolled away out of earshot. "But I believe we must keep up appearances given the article." He grimaced. "You did see it, I presume?"

Elizabeth looked at the ermine muff encasing her hands and nodded. "I did. This invitation was a good idea. Papa was…not pleased."

"I imagine he was not." A muscle worked in Jasper's jaw as he steered his matching chestnut bays toward the park where people had already begun to congregate, some on horseback, others walking. "I'm afraid my reputation has made the rumor all the more scandalous."

Ever since Elizabeth first heard of Lord Darington, she knew he had a reputation. But she also didn't entirely know in what capacity he'd earned that reputation, or why. After all, someone like Jillian had been rumored to run away from marriage due to a lack of commitment, when really her finicky approach toward potential grooms had more to do with her father insisting on who she marry.

Elizabeth's hands were sweating in the muff and she pulled them out to let the cold air wash over her damp palms. "What is it you've done?"

Jasper snapped a look of shock at her. "I beg your pardon?"

This was not a polite conversation, she knew. However, her name was tied to this man until the engagement could be broken.

She cleared her throat. "If I'm to be the subject of gossip, I should like to be privy to the things you've done, to better arm myself against the rumors."

This time when he looked at her, there was something appraising in his expression, as if in appreciation of the logic she presented.

He nodded. "Very well, though I caution this is not an appropriate conversation to be having with a lady."

Elizabeth squared her shoulders, preparing herself for whatever depravity he might throw her way. "I might be clumsy, but I'm not fragile."

He hesitated, and that is when Elizabeth's imagination took flight. There had been bits and pieces of gossip she'd heard throughout the years of scandalous couplings by others. They all flooded back now. Affairs done out of doors where the couple could be seen, lacy attire that showed more than it hid, mouths going where they had no place being.

Despite everything in her upbringing reminding her that she ought to be repulsed by such things, a delicious heat hummed between her legs, creating an intriguing throb that made her want to rub her thighs together.

"You are warned that as a reader, I have an overactive imagination and your silence only feeds a vast array of possibilities..." She arched her eyebrow at him in a similar expression he so often gave her.

Jasper guided the carriage onto the path with the others, and joined the slow procession of nobility showcasing their grand carriages, prize horses, and elegant clothing. Those strolling by gazed up at the carriage, witnessing Jasper and Elizabeth making their very public appearance.

He looked at her and smiled at the quirk of her brow. "Very well, but I'll not be accused of corrupting your innocence." His voice was quiet as he spoke, keeping their conversation private.

"You needn't worry about me, my lord." Elizabeth smiled. "I am well aware of society's gossip."

~

JASPER SHIFTED IN THE SEAT, no longer feeling the chill of the early March wind against his cheeks.

In truth, he was not concerned about shattering Elizabeth's innocence by telling her of his past. As she stated, she was aware of the ton's propensity toward salacious gossip, and surely that was more sordid than anything he'd done.

No, his hesitation came from a place of fear, that she might see for herself that he was a disappointment. But she was staring at him with expectation, silence filling the space between them as she waited for his reply.

He cleared his throat. "When I went on my grand tour, I had an exceptional number of lovers."

She lifted her brows. "Is that all?"

He mirrored her shock. "You aren't scandalized by my debauchery?"

"Don't all men do that?"

"Not to the extent I did."

"Were your lovers truly so great in number that you're still referred to as a rake?"

He looked away, not wanting to see her reaction. "Enough to warrant the attention of others, and news of my exploits made its way back to England's shores."

"Were they..."

She hesitated, and he glanced at her in time to see her press her lips together. "Were the women innocents?"

He frowned, hating that she would even think such a thing of him.

"Never," he replied firmly. "They were widows and women for whom marriage was not their intention. I would never..." he shook his head. "I've vowed to never touch an innocent woman."

She studied him for a quiet moment. "I am an innocent woman."

God, she was. Sweet and pure.

Everything he was not.

"And I will not touch you," he vowed.

She looked toward a cluster of young women walking by in heavy cloaks, the brim of her hat obscuring her expression so he could not see what she made of his reply. The sounds of multiple conversations and the clop of horse hooves on the path filled the space previously occupied by their conversation.

She slid her hands from her muff and shifted in the carriage toward him. "Why did you do it?"

"I was young," he replied simply.

She shook her head. "If what you did was excessive, the reason was more than youth."

He considered her words, the depth to them. The stark truth she was asking him to lay bare.

Her wide blue eyes searched his. "What were you trying to forget?"

His breath caught and his heart thundered in his chest. Did she truly read him so easily? When even his own parents had turned a blind eye to him for the whole of his life, did she truly see so deeply into his soul?

A longing to tell her the truth burned in his chest like a glowing ember. To confess how his father blamed him for his mother's death. How his brother's death had been his fault.

How he'd let down everyone and found himself alone, rejected, unloved, and empty. How every woman he took to his bed, in the hopes of filling that void, had failed.

"I was trying to forget how awful London was and how much I dreaded going back," he jested. A half-truth, for he did truly regret having to return.

Especially after his father died and all that awaited him was a vacant house, a title never meant to be his, and a mountain of regret.

Elizabeth's emotions were shuttered from him as she nodded and offered a placating smile. Clearly, she was not fooled by his flippant reply.

That she saw him, truly saw him, was at once both a relief and entirely terrifying.

The night at Almack's was as tedious as always to Elizabeth. Dressing up, putting on airs for the sake of those around her, being subjected to the dry cake and watery lemonade that was served week after week after week. Elizabeth would far rather be home, curled up on the right-hand side of the sofa with a new book in her hands and a hot cup of tea at her side.

Her friends usually made the miserable experience tolerable, only this time Lucy had begged off with an illness that was undoubtedly feigned, and Amy was tending to one of her sisters who was truly unwell. Even Jillian, who generally remained at Elizabeth's side, was dancing with another young gentleman her father thought would suit her.

The poor thing had been promised she could choose her own husband this year, but her father hadn't stopped sending his choices her way at every opportunity.

At least now, Elizabeth could readily decline offers to dance as she was engaged. While, yes, she could still dance, her need to impress men was no longer necessary to please her mother as Elizabeth no longer had to find a viable suitor.

For now, at least.

She did not want to think of what lay in her future. The dissolution of her engagement, the scandal that would ensue, searing through the gossip pages, and her inevitable re-entry into the marriage mart—a slab of used meat placed back on the shelf, as it were.

And giving up Jasper…

She had thought about him often, more than she should. Especially after the conversation in the carriage. He had been honest with her about his reputation, a rake with scruples. Another thing she could not free from her mind was his promise that he would never touch her.

Despite his vow, she could think of nothing else at night. In dark privacy of her bedchamber, she imagined what his fingers might feel like as they whispered across her skin, wondered at the heat of his lips that often grazed the back of her hand and what they might feel like as they explored other areas of her body. Her neck, her mouth, perhaps even her breasts.

A delicious warmth spread through her body, flooding her cheeks with a blush that made her look down at her toes, fearful someone might be able to see into her wicked thoughts.

The music began to slow, as did the dancers in preparation for the song to end. Elizabeth straightened, eager for Jillian to return, to provide ample distraction from thoughts of Jasper.

He'd been the perfect gentleman in his attempt to make everyone believe he was genuine in their engagement. The day after their carriage ride, there had been a new bouquet of flowers, tulips this time, a delicate blush pink that he said reminded him of the gown Elizabeth wore when they went to Hyde Park. The following day had been brilliant yellow daffodils that brightened the room.

That very morning had been yet another bouquet—white roses with stems and leaves of the darkest green.

Jillian's newest unwanted suitor guided her toward Elizabeth, a pompous grin on his face as he glanced about, apparently eager for people to witness them together.

The man had no idea how little Jillian liked his person, not that finding out would deflate his engorged ego.

A glance at the clock indicated the time was very nearly eleven, when the doors to Almack's would shut, barring any further attendees that evening.

Disappointment flickered in Elizabeth. She had hoped Jasper might make an appearance.

It was likely foolish to harbor such hopes, and yet her gaze wandered toward the door just as a pair of footmen approached to close it to late arrivals.

"I don't require lemonade, but thank you," Jillian's voice pulled Elizabeth's focus from the door and back to her friend.

Jillian's dance partner hesitated at the rejection, his mouth opening as if he meant to make another offer, further postponing his departure.

"Good evening, my lord," Lady Jillian said firmly. "Thank you for the dance."

He nodded, his smile tight as he spun round and left Jillian in peace.

"That was like trying to scrape something sticky from the bottom of my shoe." She puffed out a breath of air that sent the delicate curls on either side of her face floating upwards. "Come, let's procure our own lemonade and hope he sees. It would do him good to know my disinclination had nothing to do with refreshment, and everything to do with him."

"So much for your father letting you choose your own husband this year." Elizabeth cast her friend a sympathetic look.

"He said I could choose, but apparently that didn't mean he wouldn't continue to send suitors my way." Jillian's gaze skimmed the crowd, as if anticipating the next assault of another dance request from yet another suitor. Her eyes caught on something and a smile teased at her lips. "Oh, Elizabeth…" There was a singsong note to her voice, a playful tease, and it pulled Elizabeth's attention to the doors.

Jasper skirted inside just as the footmen put their hands on brass handles to seal them shut.

Elizabeth's heart knocked against her ribs. Jasper had come after all.

JASPER WAS NOT OFTEN in attendance at Almack's and only went when coerced by friends. But not tonight. Tonight he arrived with purpose, and it had everything to do with Elizabeth.

Ranford approached Jasper as he entered the stuffy establishment, much to the irritation of the footmen attempting to close the great doors.

Jasper gave them an easy smile even as he breathed a sigh of relief at having made it just minutes before eleven, when the doors would close.

"You just made it." Ranford lifted his dark brows. "I'm surprised to see you here at all."

Before Jasper could answer, his gaze was already searching the room, seeking Elizabeth.

And locating her immediately. As if he knew where to find her, drawn by intent alone.

Elizabeth chatted with Lady Jillian, each of them frosted in a pastel frock. Elizabeth was in blue, a delicate, pale color that made her skin look like cream in the candlelight.

"Ah, maybe I am not so surprised," Ranford amended. "Felicitations on your engagement. Lady Elizabeth is one of the kindest women I know." He took a breath, as though he meant to speak and then thought better of it.

Jasper regarded his friend with the lift of a brow. "What is it you mean to say?"

Ranford glanced at Elizabeth. "I hope your intentions with her are true, my friend. She is a good woman."

Anger lashed through Jasper at the implication that he might harbor ill will toward Elizabeth. Why did everyone seem to think he intended her harm? "I don't debauch women. You know that."

"I also know how you have watched her in the last two years." Ranford put his hands up, palms open in surrender. "If you say to trust you, I will. Now stop wasting your time with me and go see to your lady."

Jasper did not need to be told twice. He made his way through the throngs of people to where Elizabeth stood with her friend. As he approached, Lady Jillian nudged Elizabeth with her elbow and Elizabeth turned to face him with her mouth parted in surprise.

"My lord, I did not expect to see you here tonight."

"I could not stay away knowing you were in attendance." He grinned at her, and a blush crept over her cheeks. "Would you care to dance?"

No sooner had the words left his mouth than he knew they were the wrong ones. If she did not want a party where she was the center of attention, she would likely not want to join him on the dance floor where they would be seen by all.

Still, she nodded, ever one to please others, and took his hand.

He led her to the dance floor as the opening chords to a waltz strummed to life. Of all the dances that might have played, he was grateful it was the waltz. They would not need to trade partners as with a quadrille or be so engaged in the movements, like with a Scotch reel. In a waltz, they could talk. They could be close.

The dance would be intimately private.

Anticipation hummed in his veins.

He drew her toward him, one arm around her slim waist, the other holding her hand in his. Their proximity was such that her delicate feminine perfume teased at his senses in the most decadent way.

"Forgive me for asking you to dance, I should have realized you didn't care for it," he said quietly before the music began.

"It is good for people to see us dancing together."

Yes, a reminder that this was for show.

"We'll make sure to give them a good performance." He winked.

A smile played over her lips. "Just keep me upright."

He tightened his hold and swirled her across the dance

floor. Her steps were sure and graceful, her wide blue gaze on his in a way that made the heat of desire coil within him.

"Thank you for the flowers," she said when they slowed.

"They were my grandmother's idea," he lied.

Why had he said that?

Perhaps because it was better than confessing he went to the florist's shop every day and hand-selected the flowers, imagining they would grace her bedchamber and wanting to select the perfect blooms.

"You put up a good façade," she replied in a tone he could not read.

"Enough that I am receiving threats." He led them into a graceful twirl.

"Threats?" she gasped.

"It appears my reputation has many concerned that I mean to use you poorly."

She gave a soft laugh. "If only they knew that *I* was using *you*."

Oh, how he wished she was using him.

The thought slammed into him before he could stop it, along with the images that flashed in his mind of precisely how he longed to be used by her.

"I'm sorry you are receiving threats," she said with more seriousness as they swept across the dance floor. "I had no idea my friends and family were so vicious."

"It is my own reputation coming back to haunt me." He smirked. "Nothing at all to do with you."

"About your reputation…" she mused.

He almost missed a step, but made up for it in just enough time to keep from tripping Elizabeth.

"You vowed never to touch me." She met his eyes, her gaze direct and bold.

Why did he feel she was about to unveil a dangerous topic?

He swallowed. "I did."

"But if you allowed yourself to." Her tongue flicked out, dampening her lips, leaving them glistening and sensual. She glanced about, as though confirming others were out of earshot. "What would you do?"

A coil of desire low in his belly tightened. Was she truly asking this here?

"I beg your pardon?" he asked.

She didn't look away, but kept that bold gaze fixed on his. "How would you touch me, Jasper?"

"I should not wish to sully your innocent mind," he replied.

It was a lie. He wanted to sully her innocent mind with every caress, every kiss, every intimate touch he wished to bestow upon her person.

Elizabeth still did not look away. "What if it is not so innocent?"

He did miss a step then, but Elizabeth did a quick half step, keeping them both upright.

She smiled. "I told you I don't always need saving."

Jasper grinned at her. "Apparently I do."

No sooner had the words left his mouth, than her feet tangled with his and he felt her tip in his hands. He tightened his hold on her, securing her body to his for an instant in an effort to keep her from falling.

She was lithe in his arms, sweet and perfect. How he longed to feel the press of her against him, naked silky skin arching against him, her bottom lip pouted out for him to kiss, to suck.

Color scorched her cheeks, and he knew she was mortified at having almost fallen before the eyes of all the ton—sharks, the lot of them. All waiting for a drop of blood so they could launch into a frenzy.

"I would start by touching the length of your neck," he said softly, knowing no one else could hear them. Knowing she needed the distraction.

Knowing he could not stop himself from obliging her in this way.

After all, he was not actually touching her. He was breaking none of his promises to himself.

Elizabeth blinked in surprise, distracted from her embarrassment just as he'd hoped she would be.

"First with my fingertips, following the lines of your throat, then the hollows of your collarbone," he continued. "Then I'd repeat that path, slowly and with my mouth."

Her lips parted as she gave a little gasp.

"I'd nudge away the fabric of your low-cut bodice." He held her tighter as they twirled with the other dancers. "You said you have a good imagination. I'll allow you to use it to fill in what I might do there."

He grinned down at her as they slowed and fell into a slow, sweeping step together. "Are you scandalized?"

"With your hands...or with your mouth?" she asked, her voice husky, sensual. Aroused.

"Both." He cast her a wicked look. "Are you thoroughly shocked?"

"I've been more so." She looked at him through her lashes. "Do go on."

A low, languid laugh escaped him. He ought to stop. He knew as much, and yet there was a part of him that wanted to fulfill her desire, to tease his own desires by letting his mind play with the idea of touching her like a match. Holding it in his hands, appreciating it, but next striking it lest he erupt into flame.

"I'd raise the hem of your skirt," he said softly. "Tracing the curve of your ankle, your calf, your knee..." They spun together, his mouth close to her ear. "Your thigh, where you tied that ribbon. Then higher, grazing my fingertips over the skin of your inner thighs."

They moved closer in the dance. "And then higher still, touching you in ways even your imagination could not fathom." He nearly ran them into another couple and managed to swirl out of their way before a collision.

"With your hands, or with..." Elizabeth swallowed.

"Or with my mouth?" Jasper finished for her.

She nodded and they turned one final time together as the music tinkled to a delicate end.

"Both," he answered before bowing to her as she curtseyed.

He could not help but notice the brilliance of her cheeks as he offered her his arm to escort her back to Lady Jillian.

"Thank you," she said in a quiet tone. "That was...most edifying."

"I hope I did not scandalize you too terribly." It was another lie. He genuinely hoped he had scandalized her terribly. That his words would hum around in her mind and follow her into sleep, the way she had done to him for so long.

She shook her head, mute as he departed.

The look on her face indeed did not reflect one of shock. Rather her soft expression and the darkness in her clear blue eyes was unmistakably one of interest.

$\mathcal{E}$lizabeth knew Jasper underestimated her imagination. Especially the innocence of her thoughts.

For she could very much picture where he would touch. In fact, that very place between her legs presently echoed her heartbeat, a low thrum of undeniable desire. One she might graze with her own fingertips that night in the privacy of her room, under the cover of night, when her thoughts always wandered toward Jasper.

"Dare I ask what your dear Earl of Darington whispered in your ear while you danced?" Jillian asked as Elizabeth joined her.

Elizabeth blinked at her friend, startled from the wickedness of her thoughts.

Jillian quirked a brow. "With that look on your face, I'm even more curious."

Heat stole over Elizabeth's cheeks. "A lady never shares what is said during a waltz."

Jillian grinned. "All I know is that every woman here practically broke their necks watching you dance, wishing he would look at them the way he looks at you. And there were more than a few men admiring you as well, especially with the flush on your cheeks after the waltz."

"It was an exerting dance," Elizabeth said innocently. "And come now…" She shook her head at her friend and lowered her voice, her gaze darting about. "You know it's all an act."

Jillian settled one hand on her hip. "Do I?"

"Indeed, you do," Elizabeth gasped, feigning affront at the mere suggestion.

"You ought to be an actress with those blushes then." Jillian winked. "He's coming this way now. I must check on my darling Papa to see which man he intends to throw me in front of next."

Before Elizabeth could protest, Jillian was gone and Jasper approached with a cup of lemonade in his hand.

"Sadly, it is without brandy." He tucked his mouth down, chagrined. "But you know how the patronesses are."

Everyone knew how the patronesses of Almack's were. Securing a voucher for the elite dance hall was already difficult enough without being caught adding liquor to their bland lemonade. And once one was evicted from Almack's, there was no hope of gaining entry again.

"I scarcely need brandy," Elizabeth countered. "And I told you that time, the brandy was Lucy's."

"So you've said." He handed her the cup, and she drank, slaking a thirst she hadn't realized she had.

A smile played on his lips as he watched her, and she understood then what Jillian had referred to. That adoration Elizabeth noticed so often now filled his gaze, as if merely observing her amused him in the most endearing manner.

She felt her own lips lift in response.

He was faking, she knew, but a warmth blossomed in her regardless, one she could not control, and she found herself leaning closer toward him, eager to be near.

She caught that familiar spice she had smelled when he'd given her his jacket.

"I like when you look at me like that," he said in a low murmur that made her skin prickle with pleasure.

"Do you?" Heavens, was she flirting?

It felt silly.

And it felt wonderful.

Freeing and effervescent. Intoxicating.

He winked. "Everyone is sure to believe us when you look at me like that."

In that one sentence, the glow in her chest snuffed out, extinguished by the reality of their situation. He was an actor and every interaction they had was just another scene.

She would do well to remember, to keep from losing her heart. Playing at this game was dangerous, and she made a vow to avoid Jasper as much as possible, despite his determination otherwise.

Elizabeth managed to put off Jasper over the course of the next several days, citing a feigned illness that had Mama in a tizzy. Even still, he managed to make his presence known, his claim staked for all to see. Delicate pink roses followed the ball.

The following day, however, was her favorite. Rather than a bouquet of hothouse flowers, there had been a paper-wrapped parcel, revealing the full three-volume set of *Sense and Sensibility*, the novel first released several years prior by the same author who had written *Pride and Prejudice*, known only as 'a lady.' A note accompanied the very generous gift:

I have it on good authority reading helps improve one's constitution. I pray your health improves soon. I miss you.
Jasper

He missed her? Did he truly, or had he written that for the sake of any prying eyes which might read the missive?

She could not deny her pulse had raced at that one small line that stuck with her through the day.

His gift had also brought with it a wave of guilt at having lied to him about being unwell. Not that it had saved her from his affection. This note, this gift—ideal for a book lover—was so deeply personal, it was nearly as intimate as the conversation they'd had with their waltz. Only this time instead of appealing to her body, he'd gone straight for her heart.

On the morning of their engagement party, three dozen crimson red roses were delivered, the fragrance scenting her room with their heady perfume.

Unavoidable—just like the man who sent them.

Grace and Kitty burst into Elizabeth's room.

"We're here to prepare you for your engagement party," Grace announced, a grin on her face.

"No matter what you say," Kitty added, her lips pursed in a mock show of determination.

"So, I can't simply wear my favorite comfortable gown?" Elizabeth nodded toward the blue silk dress she genuinely had considered. It was a year out of fashion, yes, but it was the least restricting of all her gowns. And it did suit her coloring nicely.

But Kitty scowled. "Do tell me you're bamming me."

Grace slid her a sardonic look. "You know she is not."

"But Mama had a new gown made just for tonight." Kitty marched over to where the gown still lay in its box and pulled the ribbon off without ceremony. She lifted the top and sucked in a breath of sheer delight. "Oh, Elizabeth, it's lovely. Truly."

"What should I wear to my own engagement party, do you think?" Grace wondered aloud, then slid a conspiratorial look at her sisters.

"Do you mean…?" Elizabeth asked.

Grace beamed and nodded. "Harold knows we have to wait until after your engagement party before we can formally announce our betrothal, but he was too eager to put it off for a moment longer."

What was left politely unsaid was how very long Grace had been forced to wait for her engagement because of Elizabeth's inability to get married.

"Mama has already begun preparing my engagement party, which will likely be in one week." Grace squealed and clapped her hands. Her cheeks were flushed with excitement, her eyes sparkling with joy.

With love.

And even as Elizabeth's heart soared for her sister, it sank for herself.

This was how a soon-to-be bride was supposed to act on the night of her engagement party. Not with dread to see her fiancé, as Elizabeth now felt.

But there was more to the sinking sensation in Elizabeth's

stomach. Once Grace's official engagement had been secured with the public party, there was no longer a need for Elizabeth and Jasper to continue with the façade of their engagement.

The time of their pretend betrothal was finally drawing to a close. And though Elizabeth knew she should be grateful, she could not stop the pinch of hurt in her chest every time she thought of losing Jasper.

She had enjoyed her time with him. The way his flirtation made her come to life and how he was not the man he portrayed to the world and how that made her want to learn even more about it. And then there were those quiet, intimate moments they'd shared together—when he'd almost kissed her, when he'd told her exactly how he'd touch her.

Grace whisked the dress from its box, startling Elizabeth from the places her mind should not go.

"Come now, Elizabeth," Grace called out. "Let's prepare you for your own handsome fiancé."

By the time the game hens had been roasted to a golden brown and the soups poured into the tureen, and the first of the guests were on their way to Langston House, Elizabeth was laced into a corset that pushed her breasts higher than nature intended, and she'd been stuffed into the gown like a Christmas goose.

Though breathing was indeed difficult, Elizabeth had to admit that once again her sisters were correct. The gown looked stunning.

Her narrow waist was impossibly tiny in midnight-blue velvet with silver beaded flowers that caught the light and sparkled. Matching silver flowers were placed in her upswept hair among the many intricate curls, so they sparkled like stars.

Her sisters admired their handiwork, appearing more than pleased with themselves, and deservedly so, as Elizabeth had to admit.

"Lord Darington won't be able to keep his eyes off of you," Kitty exclaimed. "It's all anyone has been speaking of lately, as it is."

"Have they?" Elizabeth murmured.

"Oh, yes," Grace agreed. "Whatever you discussed during the waltz had everyone talking."

Elizabeth's face flushed. She thought of that conversation far too often. Mostly at night when she lay in her bed alone and his words whispered back to her, silky, sinful. Those were the times she let her fingertips trail over her inner thighs, pretending they were his, setting her body alight with a longing she did not know how to quench. She'd even been so bold as to stroke the seam between her legs, finding herself damp and hot, the pressure of her touch almost too exquisite to bear.

A knock came from the door, and Mama entered to announce the party was about to begin, sparing Elizabeth from having to answer Grace's question.

BESS WAS BEAMING the entire carriage ride to Langston Place.

Truth be told, Jasper was rather excited himself. He had been enjoying his engagement with Elizabeth, and missed her the last two days they had not seen one another.

He knew she'd been unwell, and he found himself

worrying over her health often, imagining her spending most of her time curled up in her bed reading, as she often said she enjoyed doing.

To that effect, he had procured the three-volume set of *Sense and Sensibility*, which had come highly recommended from the bookshop owner.

Jasper was becoming one of those ridiculous sods who fawned over a woman, but he didn't care. After all, it was all for show.

Wasn't it?

Jasper alighted from the carriage and gave his arm to Bess, leading her into Langston Place. The townhouse didn't have the ornate opulence of Darington Place, not that it was poorly appointed by any means. But in contrast, it was comfortable, lived in, in the way that suggested a family who loved one another resided inside, with thick pile rugs and tables crowded with vases and walls laden with portraits and paintings. There was a cozy warmth to the building that made it feel far more a home than the expansive halls of Darington Place, where the only thing that rang out louder than the footsteps was the silence.

Jasper and his grandmother joined Lord and Lady Langston to receive the guests just as Elizabeth descended the stairs.

She was exquisite in a dark-blue gown, sparkling with bits of silver as if she'd shone down from a moonbeam. A veritable goddess of the night.

And she would be standing by his side.

His fiancée.

He straightened taller. Tonight of all nights, he wanted to be worthy of her. Or at least appear he was.

"Doesn't she, Jasper?" Bess asked.

Jasper turned to his grandmother. "I beg your pardon?"

"I think he's quite besotted." Bess chuckled indulgently. "Doesn't your fiancée look lovely?"

"Absolutely beautiful," he answered earnestly.

Elizabeth watched him with her arresting blue eyes, never taking them off him, even as she flushed in pleasure at his words.

The receiving line was endless, when all he wanted to do was open the celebration by dancing with her.

Finally, Lord Langston addressed the room, announcing their engagement in his booming voice, beaming with pride when he looked at his daughter.

And casting one of warning to Jasper when his face was turned from the crowd. A message well-received. Again.

"Shall we dance, dearest?" Jasper asked Elizabeth.

Trepidation showed on her face.

He offered his hand to her and vowed in a voice only she would hear, "All will be well."

In truth, Jasper had been looking forward to dancing with her since their waltz.

In fact, he thought about that waltz far too bloody often.

He only hoped she did too.

Elizabeth accepted his hand as her friends and her parents all exchanged grins with one another. For Bess's part, she watched them with sparkling eyes, the look of joy on her face such that it nearly broke Jasper's heart.

This, Jasper realized, this was precisely the reason Elizabeth had gone along with the engagement party she did not want. Every smile turned in their direction came at the cost of her comfort, of her own desires, and judging from the look of love on her face as she regarded them, she had no regrets.

This joy would be short-lived, but at least they could give them tonight.

And at least there was time for Jasper and Elizabeth to enjoy each other until their engagement came to an end.

"Tell your grandmother I said thank you for all the flowers," Elizabeth said with a side look at him.

"She'll be delighted," Jasper answered. "Which have been your favorite?"

"Do you even know which ones have been sent to my home?" She teased.

And he did. Every blossom, every delicate stem, touched first by his own fingertips to be bestowed to her.

Pink roses made him recall the beauty of her sweet blushes. The purple irises that reminded him of the cast of her blue eyes in the moonlight. And red roses for the romance of the evening.

Even if theirs was a fake engagement, he could still be a romantic, could he not?

"The books," she answered. "Though I believe those might have come from you."

"I recall you had mentioned when you and my grandmother had spoken at dinner that you had enjoyed *Pride and Prejudice.*" Jasper recalled every scrap of conversation from their dinner that night. "Once I learned *Sense and Sensibility* was also by 'a lady,' I had to purchase it for you. I do hope you've recovered from your illness?"

"I truly loved the books and have already started reading them. And I'm much improved, thank you." She slid her gaze from his and he had the distinct feeling she was lying.

Had she ever been ill at all?

But would she truly feign it to avoid him?

Before the discomfort of the idea could settle over him, she continued. "The tulips have been my favorite. They're such lovely flowers. Not that the rest are not. Certainly, the bouquet today was the most impressive."

As it was meant to be.

Jasper merely smiled as they took their positions on the dance floor.

The crowd went silent.

A waltz.

Of course.

Elizabeth's mouth parted and he knew, *he knew*, she was remembering last time.

He put his hand on her narrow waist and clasped his hand with hers. "You truly do look beautiful."

"I can scarcely breathe in this corset, if I'm being entirely honest." Despite her deprecation, there was a pleased smile on her lips as she spoke.

"Perhaps you will be more comfortable when the corset is removed." His mouth went dry at the prospect.

"Are you trying to live up to your reputation?" Her lips curled around the tease, and he felt the familiar heat of desire tighten inside him.

"Do you want me to?" He shouldn't have asked such a thing. And yet he was desperate to hear her answer.

Her eyes searched his, and suddenly they were dancing in a room with no one else in it. His entire world whittled away around them, until only the two of them remained.

"Would it matter if I did want you to?" she asked.

Yes. Yes, it mattered more than anything in the world.

But whatever he might have said in ready reply dissolved on his tongue as he imagined breaking his vow to touch her. How he might tug the dress from her body, stripping away the tight corset to kiss the prints marring her slender back from where the lacings hugged uncomfortably against her skin.

"Except you don't touch virgins," she said, her voice husky as he twirled her in the dance.

Good God, had she meant that to sound like a challenge thrown at his feet?

She met his gaze and lifted her lips in a sensual grin.

And promptly tripped.

he waltz could not end quickly enough. Especially not when the entire room had seen Elizabeth trip. This was precisely the reason she never danced. She couldn't bring herself to look at Jasper, not when she fully expected the same sort of exasperated expression Mama threw her way after a bout of clumsiness. The kind of look that implored Elizabeth to be more mindful.

"I'm sorry if I embarrassed you," she whispered under her breath as they walked from the dance floor. "And thank you for catching me."

He had been quick with holding her upright as her feet confused themselves with each other. There had been a small gasp from the audience behind her, proof that there had, in fact, been witnesses.

"I wasn't embarrassed." There was a nonchalance to Jasper's tone that pulled Elizabeth's attention toward his face.

Surely he was not serious. Her parents, who loved her dearly, were always flushing with humiliation when her clumsiness plagued her in public settings. Except that Jasper looked absolutely serious.

Still assessing his demeanor, she cautiously said, "You weren't?"

He shrugged. "People trip. It certainly is not the end of the world. If people take such stock in trivial matters, their lives are small indeed."

Elizabeth had never thought of it that way before. But he was right—a little slip-up on her part mattering so much to the gossips really was quite ridiculous.

"I will always catch you, Elizabeth." He gazed at her with those fathomless dark eyes.

And in the way that he made that vow to her, she knew he would.

The corner of his mouth quirked upward. "Not that you need my protection, of course."

She smiled in reply. "Of course."

"I confess, there is part of me that cannot help but protect sometimes." There was a note of sadness in his gaze, and she didn't dare speak in the hopes he might continue voicing his thoughts.

"I minded my older brother," he said. "Benjamin was always ill, and my parents, well, essentially forced me to." He gave a mirthless chuckle. "But I have a horse, a great powerful stallion of a horse, with a glossy black coat and mane. He was wild when I bought him, hence his name, Devil's Snare." A light touched his eyes as he spoke, and Elizabeth found herself wanting to meet Devil's Snare. To know another thing that Jasper cared for so greatly, outside of his grandmother, for whom he held such obvious affection.

"My first stable master had no patience for Devil," Jasper

continued. "I found him once applying a whip in a barbarous way." He caught himself and looked around. "Not that this is appropriate conversation for an engagement party."

"We aren't one for conventional or appropriate conversations," Elizabeth rushed, worried he might stop speaking. "Please do go on."

The corner of his lip quirked up and he gave a subtle nod. "I grabbed the whip from his hand and found he'd cut poor Devil right on the chest. I released the stable master, replacing him with someone else, who I knew to have a gentle hand. That slice of the whip left a scar on his chest, the only mar to his pristine coat. Even with the new stable master, I took the remainder of Devil's training on myself. You'd never know he was such a beast to handle with how gentle he is with me now. He even runs to me from the field when he hears my voice."

Elizabeth could imagine a massive horse trotting to the stable like a puppy and chuckled. "He sounds like the most delightful devil I've ever heard of."

"More so than me?" Jasper lifted his brows suggestively.

Elizabeth covered her mouth with her hand to hide her laugh.

He opened his mouth to say something else when Lord and Lady Gentry approached. Lady Gentry's dress was tufted in wispy feathers that fluttered about her person as she effused her felicitations at their engagement and touted her own efforts in helping to spread the word of their love.

Behind Lord and Lady Gentry, the wallflowers waiting in line with their parents to offer their heartfelt affection and well-wishes. But as Lady Gentry was speaking, it did not escape Elizabeth's notice that Jasper's grandmother stopped by the wallflowers, gathering them around her as they all spoke in low tones.

What were they on about?

Before Elizabeth could think on it, Lord and Lady Gentry took their leave and Jillian's father, the Duke of Harting, strode forward to take their place with Jillian in tow.

"I should hope my own daughter will be lucky enough to find a beau with whom she is so compatible, sooner rather than later." The duke's words were meant more as a barb to his own daughter than a positive statement for Elizabeth and Jasper.

Jillian, who was entirely used to her father's biting comments on her lack of matrimonial interest, hugged Elizabeth and then gazed between her and Jasper. "You truly are such a handsome couple. I imagine your children will be quite stunning."

Elizabeth's eyes nearly bulged from their sockets.

What would possess Jillian to say such a thing when she knew the truth of their pretend engagement?

Mr. and Mrs. Honeyfield came next with Amy between them. Mrs. Honeyfield had the same golden hair and warm brown eyes as her daughter, her expression just as loving and kind, as she wished Elizabeth and Jasper happiness in their union.

"I cannot wait to see you married," Amy added eagerly after her mother spoke. "Elizabeth will be an exquisite bride."

Jasper smiled at Elizabeth, admiration shining in his eyes. "That she will."

Truly, he was far too good at this acting business.

And what on earth had gotten into Amy to say such a thing?

Next came Lucy with her parents. The Beauchamps offered similar praise as the Honeyfields, only this time Elizabeth found herself tensing when it came time for Lucy to say something about the engagement.

"Do you have a date set yet?" Lucy asked. "I've heard it rumored you're keen on a springtime wedding, which would mean we only have a month or so to plan."

Elizabeth's mouth fell open.

"I believe that is what my grandmother and Lady Langston are conspiring to achieve," Jasper replied easily.

Elizabeth trained her features to keep from showing how appalled she was at her friends' bizarre statements.

On and on the line of people went, ready to congratulate Elizabeth and Jasper on their engagement. Through every new felicitation, Jasper remained the consummate actor, playing the lovestruck earl who had been so taken by his esteem for her that he had not been able to help his spur-of-the-moment proposal.

It was a romantic tale to be sure. One Elizabeth would have swooned over to have read in a book.

One she might have even secretly wished for herself had she not been party to it now, and knowing it to be nothing more than a scheme.

When, finally, the crowd of well-wishers dwindled and the last few people offered their affection, Jasper turned to Elizabeth. "Would you like to take some air, my darling?"

The idea of going outside, away from the press of people, free from the prying gazes, made her want to sigh in relief. "I would absolutely love that."

He offered her his arm. "I assumed as much."

Perhaps that was what was hardest for her about the ruse.

His attention to her was so exact, he knew what she needed, sometimes before even she did. Such a level of care was far too difficult to brush away as merely acting.

And yet it was, she reminded herself. Even still, there was a part of her that wanted to believe it as readily as she did the love stories she read about in her novels.

Jasper led her through the room toward the rear patio overlooking the garden, and opened the door for her.

The bite in the air was ice cold, but the chill was a reprieve against the heat in her cheeks, and the quiet of the dormant garden was bliss after the cacophonous noise of the engagement party.

"You are so good at speaking with others." Elizabeth glanced around the empty area, confirming that they were indeed alone. "At being charming."

She tensed, knowing this was a start to what she needed to tell him, that Grace was going to be having her own engagement party soon. That their faux engagement would be coming to an end.

Jasper took off his jacket and placed it around her shoulders. The wool was heavy and warm with the heat of his body and carried that sensual spicy fragrance that was becoming so wonderfully familiar to her.

He studied her for a long moment. "Being charming is easy to do with a woman such as yourself."

She gave a shy laugh. "You don't have to pretend with me."

"I'm not pretending, Elizabeth. You are beautiful."

He was watching her with that dark gaze again, making her body burn for something he promised he would never give her.

"It's the dress," she admitted. "Mama and my sisters insisted—"

"No." Jasper stepped closer to her. "You have always been beautiful."

She opened her mouth, uncertain how to respond to such flattery. He continued, sparing her from having to reply. "I first noticed you at Lord Whimbley's ball two years ago. You were the most beautiful woman there."

Most beautiful woman there?

Now he was going too far. Didn't she tell him he didn't have to pretend with her?

She shook her head. "You must have been mistaken. That was likely not me."

"You were standing against the wall looking as though you were trying to blend into it." A secret smile hovered on his lips.

"Very well," she conceded. "Yes, that does sound like me."

"When your friends approached, your face bloomed with delight. You were radiant. This quiet, gentle woman clearly wanting to be anywhere but at that ball—which admittedly was tedious as far as they go. But for your friends, you came to life. I've never seen someone care so much for others, or be embraced with such affection. I couldn't take my eyes off you. I couldn't stop thinking about you."

His words were a spell woven around her, intoxicating as they obliterated the shreds of doubt from her thoughts. She wanted to believe what he was saying. Desperately so.

"You couldn't?" Elizabeth swallowed. "Why didn't you approach me?"

"After you rejected every man who approached you?"

She flushed.

He stepped closer, his gaze serious and intense. "But even if I could bring myself to, women like you aren't meant for men like me."

Her breath was coming too fast, making her head spin. "Whatever do you mean?"

"Respectable ladies…" His eyes were on her lips and suddenly they felt dry. She darted her tongue out to moisten them and his nostrils flared.

"Because of your reputation?" she whispered.

His jaw flexed. "Yes."

"Because you vowed not to touch me."

He breathed a moment, his breath a hard pull in and out. "Yes."

Something niggled at the back of her mind. The reminder that she had to tell him their charade was nearly up. And yet, here was Lord Darington telling her he'd always found her beautiful, had always noticed her. This man who she had dreamed of for too long had wondered about her.

And had desired her.

Surely, they could pretend just a bit longer.

Only this time, she wanted to fall head over heels into the fantasy. To set aside her skepticism and play the lead role alongside him.

"What if…" Her heart thundered in her ears. Was she truly going to say this. "What if I told you I wanted you to touch me?"

He inhaled sharply. "I can't."

If she thought such words were a rejection, she was mistaken. For the way he continued to watch her with his dark, steady gaze, begged her to press him.

"What if we pretend?" She caught him by the hand and

eased backward to the building, obscuring them in a cloak of shadows. "What if we pretend we will be wed in a fortnight, that reputation does not stand between us, that soon all intimacy will be shared with one another."

Elizabeth's heel hit the wall, and she stopped, locking her eyes on Jasper.

"That is a lot of pretending." But even as he said it, he leaned over her, bracing his body with an arm on either side of her.

"I have a very active imagination," she whispered.

"So you've said," he murmured.

She tilted her face toward his. "Kiss me."

Was she begging?

She didn't care. All she knew was that she wanted—needed —the heat of his mouth on hers.

He hesitated a moment, long enough she was certain he would deny her request. Disappointment chilled inside her and then suddenly he moved, grasping her firmly but gently at the back of her head and lowered his lips to hers.

JASPER KNEW he shouldn't be kissing Elizabeth, but her mouth was so sweet under his, so soft, so yielding.

She had goaded him with her teasing earlier during the dance, and now with her throaty, whispered plea, all but begging him to kiss her.

Good God, how could he not?

His mouth moved over hers, claiming her lips as if he could make her entirely his with that act of one simple kiss.

But no, there was nothing simple about it.

Not in the way he possessively cradled the back of her head against his palm, or in how his body bowed over hers, drawn toward her beauty, her undeniable sensuality as she sweetly tormented him with a flirtation he could not deny.

He kissed first that full lower lip he'd spent far too much time thinking about, then her top lip, before capturing them together. She returned his kiss, her movements slow with inexperience and determined with need.

It was that need which spurred him beyond that one kiss.

For truly that was what he had intended.

One simple kiss to placate her request. To slake his curiosity of how she might taste.

One kiss was not enough, damn it.

He ran his tongue over the seam of her lips, sampling her. Encouraging her.

Her mouth parted and he dipped his tongue inside, brushing the tip of hers with his own.

A soft moan escaped her—a breathy whimper, a lusty plea for more.

God, such a sound could fell a man.

He sucked her full lower lip into his mouth, scraping it gently with his teeth before freeing it to tease her with his tongue once more.

This time she met the probe of his tongue with a curious parry of her own. Her arms curled around his back, drawing her toward him, arching against his body where his lust burned like the Spanish summer sun.

His body was on fire with longing for her, the breath caught in his chest against the thundering of his heart, and his cock was so damn hard, it nearly hurt.

"Touch me," Elizabeth said against his mouth.

He froze. Had she really said such a thing?

She arched against him again. "Touch me, please."

A voice in the back of his mind reminded him they were on the patio, where any person could walk out and find them in such a compromised position. But he had never been one to follow caution...

One touch.

That's all he would do.

His mouth trailed down the slender column of her neck, to where the corset pushed her firm breasts up toward his eager lips. He ran his fingertips along the low edge of the corset, whispering against petal soft skin.

Elizabeth whimpered, pushing her generous breasts toward him.

Jasper played his fingertips over that corset, hating how it hid her from him. Wanting to see her. To taste her.

Putting his thumb against her sensual breast, he nudged the fabric down with his other hand, freeing one rosy nipple which immediately pebbled in the cold. He leaned over her, closing his mouth around it, tracing the peaked shape with his tongue before flicking it in a way that made her grip his head to her bosom.

She was a responsive lover, the type he loved the most, whose gasps and moans told him what she liked. So that he could do even more.

Her hips were arching toward him, and he obligingly eased his knee between her legs.

He knew the moment her sex grazed over his thigh for she moaned with great delight and shifted over him again and again.

How he longed to touch even more. To sample that sweet place so desperate for relief.

But instead, he straightened and carefully tucked her breast back into her corset.

Her chest heaved with her frenzied breathing and her eyes sparkled like diamonds of desire in the darkness. "Please..." she whispered.

With a groan, he captured her lips once more, unable to stop as he knew he should.

She kissed him back with enthusiastic zeal that pushed away any rational thought. He drew the glove off his right hand and caught a fistful of her skirts with the left.

He kissed her with abandon, feeling the smooth fullness of her lips on his, the warmth of her breath as she moaned into his mouth. Meanwhile, he drew up her skirt with one hand, just to the knee, just enough to slip his hand beneath.

His fingers found the smooth silk of her stockings, the glossy length of ribbon tying it just above her knee, likely a perfect match to the one in the pocket of his robe at home.

How he wished they were alone, that he could pull off those ribbons, free those stockings, and pull the dress from her body, revealing all of her to him.

But this would do for now.

Her skin was hot against his cold hands, smooth as gossamer. She panted as his fingers crept higher up her legs, seeking the source of her need.

He reached the apex of her thighs, to the cleft in between. With the lightest of touches, he dragged his fingertips over her.

She gasped against his lips and her knees buckled. He

grabbed her with his left arm even as his fingertips stroked against her once more, this time more firmly.

A whimper sounded in her throat.

"You must be quiet," he murmured in her ear, and she buried her face against his shoulder.

He held her thus, letting her cries of surprised delight and pleasure melt against his body, resonating in his ears. She was so damn wet against his fingers, hot and eager.

So ready for him that he had to clamp down on his back teeth to stave off his own longing.

All he wanted in this moment was her pleasure.

His thumb found the swollen nub and he circled it slowly at first, then with more haste. Her breath hitched and he knew she would not take long to bring to release.

God, how he appreciated an easy lover.

Her body tensed, so close to the brink.

He pressed his mouth to her throat, kissing her gently as his fingers worked over her. "Come for me, my love," he growled.

She stiffened, and her gasps of euphoria were absorbed with his lips as her sex spasmed against his fingers.

An exhale shuddered from her as she drew back, her gaze wide and blinking with wonder. "I...I had no idea it could be like that."

He removed his hand, letting her skirts fall back into place as he eased his glove back over his hand, his fingers still damp with her arousal.

"That is only the beginning, dearest." He grinned at her, wishing he could show her every element of pleasure he'd learned in his youth. Only now he would appreciate them so much more with a woman he found as intriguing and respectable as he did beautiful and desirable.

But tonight was for her.

To show her passion, but maintain her innocence.

Because she was not his. And he would do well to remember that.

Someday, some other man would marry her. Someone else who would part her thighs as she took him into her, having what Jasper could not.

A spike of jealousy drove through him.

Because even if he knew he didn't deserve her, he wanted to be that man, damn it.

"We should return inside," he said abruptly. "Or people will speculate over our prolonged absence."

Elizabeth nodded, her cheeks flushed. Her lips were swollen from their kisses, her eyes still bright with desire.

One need take only one look at her to know what they had been on about.

"I should not have done that." He ran a hand through his hair.

"Why not?" She asked.

"Because you're an innocent. I have no right to…to do what I did."

Most women might become emotional at such a reply, but Elizabeth just tilted her head, her approach pragmatic as it always seemed to be. "Then why did you?"

Her question was not accusatory, but asked in genuine interest.

"Because I could not help myself." He sighed. "I can never seem to help myself around you."

And that very much was the problem.

He liked the time he spent with Elizabeth, he loved the way she respected him when others did not, how she'd wanted to hear *why* he had a sordid past rather than judging him for it. He liked how she made him feel like he could be a better man with her. And even though he knew she despised her clumsiness, he found it endearing.

In that moment, Jasper realized he did not wish to end their engagement. That perhaps they might take the risk to bring the engagement to fruition.

But now was not the time to bring up marriage, with her eyes starry and fevered from orgasm. No, tomorrow would be better. When he called on her following the engagement party.

He would tell her then of his wish to marry her, and hoped to God that this real proposal ended in a *yes*.

12

Elizabeth practically floated into bed that night, her body still warm and humming from Jasper's touch. Morning, however, brought a stark reality, when fantasy gave way to the truth of reality. The night before had been about roles acted out like fantasies—a fairy tale.

With Grace's engagement party soon approaching, there was no more need for pretending.

Although the way he had spoken the night before, perhaps he was not pretending. She would watch his face as she spoke, to gage his reaction.

Resolved, Elizabeth pulled herself from bed as her maid entered, preparing herself to begin her day, and steeling herself for the inevitable visit from Jasper that would surely follow on the heels of their engagement party.

When Jasper's daily hothouse flowers arrived, they came delivered in Jasper's own hands. Lovely pink and white tulips, their waxy petals opened and full, on fragile stems. He offered them with a charming smile. "I believe you stated these were your favorite."

Grace accompanied them in the drawing room, tucked into the corner overlooking the garden, her attention fixed on a bit of sewing. The favor was one Elizabeth had repaid when Scorbridge called on Grace, each sister affording the other as much privacy as possible under society's strict rules.

But even that extra privacy was not as much as Elizabeth wished she and Jasper could have with what needed to be said. Still, one must make do.

Jasper sat beside Elizabeth, his hands absent gloves, his long, tapered fingers calling her attention. Her thoughts raced back to the night before, what he had done with those fingers. How skillfully he had played her body. How readily she'd melted at his touch, under what he'd done to her.

All night she had wondered what more he could do to her.

He followed her gaze and gave a lopsided grin. "Last evening was memorable."

Heat scorched her cheeks. "Indeed." Her voice caught with an embarrassing croak, and she quickly cleared her throat, reaching for her teacup.

"However..." He glanced at where Grace had all but turned her back to them. "I should not have done what I did."

"You regret it."

Something played in his eyes, unreadable, but concerning. "Regret? No, there is much more to it than that."

A tap of panic resounded in the back of Elizabeth's mind. This was where he reminded her they were just feigning being lovers, that the charade had gone too far. That she was a fool to try to read into anything else.

"You see..." He shifted on the sofa, his words halting as if he had difficulty piecing together exactly what he wanted to say.

And Jasper was never at a loss. Not like this.

No doubt he was trying to let her down easy.

Elizabeth set aside her teacup with a hasty clatter. "My sister will be having her engagement party soon. In just over a week."

Jasper blinked. "I'm sure Scorbridge will be immensely pleased to finally be making their engagement official."

"Precisely." Elizabeth sat nearer to the edge of the seat, lowering her voice. "And that means we need not be engaged much longer."

His eyes narrowed shrewdly. "I see."

But what did that mean?

"The entire point of ensuring our engagement was to allow Grace to finally marry the man she loves," Elizabeth babbled on in a bid to see his expression change into something readable. "Once they have publicly announced their engagement, the ruse of our impending union is no longer necessary. It will free you up to find a lady more suitable for you that can give your grandmother the great-grandchildren she wants."

His face went blank for the span of several moments before finally breaking out in a smile. "What a relief."

Her heart broke at such a statement. His reaction jabbed at a place inside her, creating a wound from what had once only been a sore spot.

She had been correct. No matter how well he played the part of lover, he did not want her.

"Yes, a relief," she echoed. "Likely we will not need to continue seeing one another as it will lay the foundation for people to see our affection for one another beginning to dissolve."

A muscle worked in Jasper's jaw, and he gave a single nod. "Of course."

Really, she made such the suggestion not entirely for the benefit of layering the story in light of their impending broken engagement, but for herself. She could not pretend a moment longer. She could not see him every day knowing that he was relieved to be done with her presence.

If she was not to be with him, she did not wish to see him at all.

Better that he move on to a woman he wanted to marry, a woman he'd genuinely asked from the onset. And better that she free up her heart to possibly find a real engagement for herself. One based on love.

After all, that's what she'd wanted since she was a young girl, despite the wallflower pact. If she was ever to marry, she wanted to find someone who would love her for her, exactly how she was.

"As to that, my lady, I suspect it would be best to take my leave." He stood and put his gloves on, somehow severing the intimacy between them with that simple action. "We cannot have people assuming we are besotted with one another." He gave her a smile that didn't reach his eyes and made her immediately miss the warmth of his affection.

How quickly he could turn off the charm, as effortlessly as he had turned it on.

Elizabeth thought she would feel better having finally done what she'd intended since the moment they'd been found in that empty study together. Except she felt worse. Far, far worse than she'd ever imagined, and she spent the better part of the day curled up in bed with the excuse of a headache.

But while she thought she might feel better the next day,

she in fact did not, going from awful to worse than awful when the usual morning delivery of hothouse flowers from Jasper did not arrive.

The absence of that bouquet was the beginning of the end, and already Elizabeth mourned the loss of the man she was never supposed to love.

The man, she strongly suspected, she absolutely *did* love.

JASPER PROWLED around Darington Place the next morning, lost in a tangle of thoughts from which there was no reprieve.

He dissected the conversation again and again, breaking it down piece by analytical piece. At no point had he shown his hand to his opponent. Surely, she could not have known he was going to propose marriage.

For years he had kept his heart sheltered by a wall, and now, he had finally begun to let that wall chip away, revealing the parts of him that were still wounded. Still raw. Still so bloody vulnerable. He had begun to let her in.

Thank God he had not yielded himself completely, lest he look the fool.

He was only glad she had ended things when she did, sparing his pride from yet another blow in life where one more might be mortally wounding.

When he finally allowed himself to show at luncheon, Bess was waiting for him with a small pile of papers. "I believe I've found the perfect baker to provide the pastries for your wedding."

Jasper's already sour mood curdled further. "There won't be a wedding."

Silence followed his announcement.

Bess lifted her brows. "There was a well-attended engagement party two nights ago that would suggest otherwise."

Jasper shook his head, not wanting to discuss it. Least of all with Bess.

"You've changed your mind about her," Bess said softly. "I worried she might be too tame for you."

"It is not me who has changed my mind," he replied. "Or rather, it is, but not in the way you mean."

"You aren't making a lick of sense." She sniffed. "I imagine there is a wild tale beneath all of this intrigue."

He scowled.

"Precisely." She poured a fresh cup of tea for herself and one for him, then settled back in her chair. "I suggest you start from the beginning."

He sighed and did exactly that, explaining how he'd gone into the study to escape all the Mamas and the debutantes they wanted to thrust in his direction.

"Well, that certainly explains why you haven't found a wife," Bess muttered, interrupting him.

"You certainly tried to hand sell me like a meat pie," Jasper fired back, still prickly.

But Bess was never offended by such things and merely smirked. "I did rather, didn't I?" She held up her hands, helpless. "Who could blame me? I was just trying to help. Anyway, on with your tale."

He continued about how Elizabeth had entered the darkened study to fix her stocking and they had been caught.

"I suppose you can find a wife like that." Bess cackled out a laugh. "A loose stocking, eh? I'm sure you didn't mind catching a peek at that."

"Bess," Jasper said in a warning tone.

"I dare say, is that a blush creeping over your cheeks?" She tapped his knee with her cane and laughed again when he shot her an irritated look.

"At least that explains the study incident the scandal sheets mentioned." She nodded encouragingly. "What happened next?"

"There's nothing that happened next." Because he was certainly not going to confess to his grandmother that he made Elizabeth come apart in his arms on the patio at their fake engagement party.

"Obviously something happened next." Bess threw her arms up and exasperation. "The way she looks at you. The way you look at her. I'm old, but I am not dead, my boy. You take my word for it, that woman wants to be your wife in earnest."

Jasper rolled his eyes, annoyed at having to recount the minute—not to mention painful—details. "Her younger sister has been wanting to become engaged, which is why Lady Elizabeth continued along with the scheme for as long as she did. Now that their engagement party is set to happen in the next week, she plans to call off our engagement."

"Which makes you feel like you are no longer needed," Bess said softly.

Her words were like a blade to his heart, slicing into him with the truth he had tried too hard to acknowledge.

"Why the devil don't we drink scotch at luncheon?" He glanced about for the footman so as to request something stronger than tea.

"Scotch put you in this mess, Jasper. That wit and charm of yours will get you out. Just tell her how you feel."

"I'm not…" Jasper ran an aggravated hand through his hair. "I'm not meant for a woman like her."

Bess put a hand on her hip, affronted. "What the bloody hell do you mean by that?"

He gave a wry smile. "Grandmothers shouldn't say *bloody hell*."

"And grandsons shouldn't change the subject when it's important. Pray tell what you mean by 'you aren't meant for a woman like her.'"

He lifted a shoulder. "I could never be good enough for her."

"That's preposterous. You're more than good enough for her, now put that out of your head." Bess patted his arm. "Do you want a hug?"

An ache blossomed in his chest for the sweet embrace of his grandmother, like she used to do when he was just a boy. After Benjamin had died, followed not long after by his mother. The soft, warm, maternal embrace that made him feel like the world was all right again.

But grown men did not need such things.

"That's unnecessary."

"Maybe for you." Bess pushed up on her cane. "But this old lady could do with a hug after learning she will no longer be receiving the great-grandchildren she's been promised." She shot him a pointed look, one meant to inspire guilt.

And blast it—she was successful.

"I'm still dying after all," she added with a careless shrug.

"You absolutely are not." With a sigh, Jasper went to his grandmother, and she wrapped her arms around him, filling his senses with that familiar rosemary scent of her. He relaxed into the embrace, taking comfort the way he'd done as a boy. "And thank God for it."

She patted his back. "You just leave this to me."

Jasper stiffened. "What do you mean by that?"

She released him, tutting as she readjusted herself upon her cane, a mischievous gleam in her eyes. "Never you mind. All will be well."

"Bess." There was a warning note to his tone. One she did not heed as she hobbled from the room. With purpose, damn it.

This would not end well.

13

The reason Elizabeth was outside on this rare sunny day that felt far too bright for her mood had nothing to do with trying to elevate her spirits, and everything to do with spending time with her friends.

She had tried to invite the wallflowers to Langston Place where they could have privacy, but they had declined—a collective effort to enjoy one of the few days of sunshine in an otherwise bitterly cold spring.

In truth, Elizabeth had not wanted to go. Even knowing she would have a lovely time, the act of preparing to go out was a most arduous, miserable task. She did not want to don a pretty frock, or have her hair styled just so, or have to put on airs while out among the ton as she confessed to her friends that the fake engagement was soon coming to an end.

The location finally convinced her in the end, which was out of the way of London's society—rather, they were on the outskirts, in a secluded section of Richmond Park. Really, the remote park was the ideal location to share such poor news, where there would be few ears to listen.

Elizabeth was the last to arrive, likely due to her lack of a desire to leave the house.

Lucy, Jillian, Amy, and even Hannah were there already. Likely this was why they had suggested the distant park, so that Hannah might join them despite her being in a delicate way. They waved in unison when they saw Elizabeth from where they all sat amid a large blanket spread upon the tender new grass, ignoring the chill in the breeze as they poured from a pot tea that would likely be cold before it could be sipped.

"What's wrong?" Amy asked as Elizabeth approached.

"Nothing," she lied quickly.

Jillian's eyes narrowed. "It is clearly not at all 'nothing.'"

"How do you always know?" Elizabeth asked, exasperated. She hadn't prepared to launch into her tale of woe so soon after joining her friends.

She had wanted some fun, some laughter, a completed distraction from the misery of her current life.

And yet they all stared at her in expectation.

She sighed. "Jasper and I have started to distance from one another so our broken engagement will look convincing. See? It is nothing." She could hear the forced brightness in her own voice that fooled absolutely no one.

"Oh, how horrible." Amy's gasp that followed seemed hollow somehow. Like a charade.

"It isn't really," Elizabeth said with false enthusiasm. "I don't have to pretend anymore. It's been dreadful if I'm entirely honest."

Not all of it. In fact, very little of it had truly been dreadful.

"But were you pretending?" Jillian asked. "You'd seemed so..."

"Happy," Lucy finished.

Elizabeth stared at her friends, at a total loss of words. They knew this would always be the outcome. With a little laugh, she tried to shrug off the weight of their words. "It was all an act, as you were well aware."

"Then you are a very good actress," Hannah said, a hand languidly stroking her large belly.

"That's my line," Amy mouthed.

"From what I've heard, I mean," Hannah added quickly.

Elizabeth frowned. "What is this about?"

"Well, you're clearly a better actor than we are," Lucy said with a flash of her brilliantly white smile. "Because you had us fooled."

"Fooled?" Elizabeth lifted a brow.

Amy took Elizabeth's hand, her palm warm despite the cold day. "That you wanted to actually marry him."

"I..." Elizabeth shook her head, the denial congealing in her throat refusing to emerge. "It isn't meant to be."

"Isn't it?" Hannah asked, a slow smile spreading on her face.

Fear shot through her, so cold, the breeze felt suddenly balmy by comparison. "What are you talking about?"

The four women shared looks, appearing far more guilty than Elizabeth cared to admit.

"What have you done?" Elizabeth demanded.

"Umm..." Amy cringed and looked over Elizabeth's shoulder.

She turned just in time to see Jasper walking up the path with his grandmother at his side.

"We may have set something into motion we cannot stop,"

Jillian answered quickly. "And we've only done it because we love you."

"And we want you to be happy," Hannah added.

Jasper and his grandmother walked up the path toward the picnic. They were nearly upon them when Jasper looked up, his gaze going past the spread of confections and tea and finding Elizabeth.

His stare held hers and the entire world seemed to stop. The wind no longer played at her hair, the chill no longer pinched her cheeks, the sun no longer glinted blindingly overhead.

There was only her and Jasper and the world of unspoken longing that pulled at her like an anchor.

"Oh my," Lady Darington cooed. "Imagine finding you ladies here."

Jasper broke off his gaze from Elizabeth to cast his grandmother a withering look. "Yes, I imagine the idea of 'needing some time away from the bustle of London' to come specifically to this park was entirely coincidental."

Lady Darington ignored him. "Lady Elizabeth, you do look lovely today."

Elizabeth had seen herself in the mirror that morning and knew she most assuredly did *not* look lovely. The shadows under her eyes stood dark against the pallor of her skin, and she'd only barely scraped herself together to appear presentable with as minimal effort as possible.

"Please, the two of you ought to join us," Amy offered.

"Yes, please do," Hannah added. "There's plenty of food."

"That is kind of you," Jasper started, just as Lady Darington beamed and spoke over him, "Don't mind if we do. Jasper, go sit by your fiancée."

Jasper only hesitated for a fraction of a moment, his jaw tight as he complied with his grandmother's request. After all, they *were* supposed to still be engaged.

Elizabeth sat down and he sank down beside her on the blanket. She cleared her throat. "Would you like some tea before it gets cold on this blustery day?"

"You mean a day that is most definitely not suited for a picnic?" he asked with a lift of his brow. "By all means."

Tension quickened in the air between them.

"Oh goodness, what is that?" Hannah exclaimed. "I believe it's a rabbit!"

Elizabeth looked toward the bushes nearby, but didn't see a rabbit.

"Indeed, it is," Lucy said. "And it's adorable."

Lucy never said words like 'adorable.'

This charade was truly ridiculous.

In fact, this charade was reminiscent of a near replica with a cat, when Lucy lured Hannah out so she might speak to Lord Brightstone when they were at odds with one another during their marriage.

"I should like to take a closer look," Lady Darington announced. "I do love rabbits."

"Of course she does," Jasper said under his breath, but even as he did, a smile pulled at his lips and he shared a look with Elizabeth.

She couldn't help but laugh and he chuckled, the wall of awkwardness crumbling as Jasper's grandmother and Elizabeth's friends hastened away after a nonexistent animal in an effort to force them together.

"Well, it appears we have been set up," Elizabeth said with a laugh.

Jasper chortled. "They did work hard to get us to this point, did they not?"

The silence fell over them once more like a blanket.

Elizabeth picked at a loose thread on the hem of her dress. "I believe they are distressed at the end of our arrangement. I told my friends, as well as I'm sure you told your grandmother."

Jasper drew in a quiet breath as if he meant to speak, then closed his mouth.

Elizabeth knew she ought to fill the conversation with something, but did not quite know what to say either.

He looked at her then—really, fully looked at her, the depth of those fathomless eyes searching her own in a way that touched her soul. "I am distressed at the end of our arrangement as well."

Had he really said that?

"I beg your pardon?" she asked, hating that her voice seemed so small and insignificant that the wind almost carried it away.

Jasper shifted so he sat directly in front of her. "I don't want our engagement to end."

Jasper watched Elizabeth for her reaction, his heart pounding.

She drew a sharp intake of breath, her eyes searching his, as if trying to seek out the truth.

With hope?

Perhaps?

There was nothing for it, but to press on.

"While our engagement may have started as a ruse, my enjoyment of our time together has been entirely real," he said. "I did not realize that until I wasn't seeing you every day."

She bit her lip. "I've enjoyed my time with you as well. And have also missed you."

He exhaled a breath, feeling his body beginning to relax.

Several feet away, Bess was huddled with Elizabeth's friends, searching for a rabbit that didn't exist.

He chuckled. "They're rather ridiculous with this pretense, aren't they?"

"I hope for their sake, they really do find a rabbit."

"Either way, I'm glad to be here with you." He looked at Elizabeth once more.

She looked awful.

Rather, she was still beautiful—she would always still be beautiful—with those lovely blue eyes that reminded him of the endless stretch of a late summer sky, and her chestnut-brown hair that gleamed in the sun. And, of course, that full bottom lip that he recalled too often, remembering how soft it felt against his mouth, his tongue.

But it was evident she had not been sleeping well. The delicate skin under her eyes was dark, bruised with exhaustion, and the energy which usually seemed so boundless that it glowed about her now seemed dulled.

His own had dulled as well, without her.

"I know we started our engagement as a façade, a means to spare your reputation and allow your sister to marry Scorbridge, but I should very much like to continue our engagement." He reached for her hand, hating the gloves they both wore that added cloth barriers to the wonderful intimacy of skin on skin.

"If we continue the engagement, you do know that your grandmother and my mother will be pushing for a springtime wedding." She looked at their hands and then back up at him. "Which means this fake engagement will lead to a very real marriage."

"I cannot imagine anyone whom I would rather marry than you." He touched her face with his free hand, the fingertips of his gloves brushing her jawline as he recalled the silken feel of her.

Her breath came more quickly. "What are you saying, Jasper?"

She was asking him to say the words aloud, to break down the final barriers he'd built around his heart. He couldn't remember the last time it had been laid so fully bare, so raw and open and vulnerable.

"I want to marry you, Elizabeth. Not as a ruse to mask a mistake on both our parts, innocent though they might have been, but in earnest. With the intention to be your husband and for you to be my wife."

Elizabeth stared at him wide-eyed, cheeks pink from either emotion or the wind that pulled at the blue ribbons of her bonnet and made them dance in the wind.

Elizabeth's friends and his grandmother had given up all pretense of finding the nonexistent rabbit and now had turned their unconcealed attention on Elizabeth and Jasper. He threw them a sardonic look and they all quickly turned away.

"Do you love me?" Elizabeth asked abruptly.

Jasper blinked. "I beg your pardon?"

"I know we've only known each other a short time and it's probably a foolish thing to ask, but, well, do you love me?" She shrugged her shoulders up to her sheepish expression, looking suddenly as though she would rather be anywhere but there.

The question took him aback.

Had he not already laid down his pride? Had he not already opened his person and his heart to rejection when he asked her to marry him in earnest?

But love?

Love?

Such an emotion was a complicated maze, a trek he could not endeavor to pursue, not when he was not sure he could ever love again. His heart was too shattered for such a thing, most of the pieces too broken to put back together. Even the few he had managed to repair for Bess were badly cracked.

He could have easily replied with a light jest, but the earnestness of her gaze told him she wanted a genuine answer. And he knew in his soul she would not like what he had to say.

"Many marriages do not begin with love," he answered finally.

Her face shuttered from him, almost a visible snapping closed of her expression. "So you do not love me."

It was not a question, but a statement. And one he could not refute.

Because he did not love her. He did not love anybody.

He held her hand more firmly in his, as if by keeping her from physically pulling away, he might do so emotionally as well. "I'm sorry, but I do not."

Her nod was stiff, but she left her hand tucked in his. "Do you think you ever could? Love me, I mean."

He gazed into her lovely blue eyes, wanting nothing more than to lose himself in them and ascribe to every notion of love and romance he'd ever known.

But he couldn't.

Love was poison, an insidious leech upon the body that drained one of reason and logic and opened oneself to exploitation. He had seen it many times in his life, not only with others, but with himself.

His mother had exploited his love to make him guard over his brother. A familiar ache stung at Jasper's heart. And when he'd failed at that, his father had turned his mother's love into something horrible, citing it for what had killed her in the end.

And putting the full blame on Jasper's shoulders.

No, he could not love again. It was far too painful.

He shook his head. "Forgive me, but I don't know if I can."

She gasped out an exhale that sounded like a choked sob and wrenched her hand from his, the connection between them severing in a way that was jarringly abrupt and left him immediately bereft.

"Then my answer is no," she said, her tone almost incredulous. "I deserve better."

And in those words, she confirmed exactly what he knew and had always known. She *did* deserve better. Someone who didn't have a stained past, someone whose heart was not so wounded that he could never open it fully again.

In this way, their soon-to-be broken engagement truly was for the best.

14

$\mathcal{S}$everal days had passed and still Elizabeth didn't know why she had demanded to hear that Jasper loved her.

No, actually, she knew exactly why.

All her life, in every book she'd ever read, in every novel that swept through her soul, there had been a man and woman who loved passionately and fiercely. And while Elizabeth had never been keen on the idea of marriage, she was certain that if she should ever find someone worthy of breaking her pact with the wallflowers, that man would love her. Truly. Passionately.

She had even offered Jasper an out, an opportunity to suggest that he might in time come to love her.

He could not even do that.

Hiccupping a sob as she closed the second installment of *Sense and Sensibility*, feeling entirely like Marianne, the tears began to fall.

Again.

She'd been a miserable wreck since the picnic, mourning

the loss of an engagement that had not yet been officially broken. Although she had sent him a missive informing him she intended to start spreading the news of her malcontent with him at Grace's engagement party, citing how ill-suited they were.

She did not want him to see the rumors in the scandal sheet and be taken aback by the gossip.

He had not replied.

When she'd sent the note, time felt like a chasm, a yawning space she did not know how she would fill. Now, Grace's engagement party was to start in an hour. The death knell for whatever it was that existed between Elizabeth and Jasper.

Companionship.

That was all it had been.

Playing at love that could never exist.

Because he could not love her.

Tears welled in her eyes again.

Heavens, she really *was* the embodiment of Marianne's character.

She closed the book, unable to read about Marianne's heartbreak when her own was so heavy.

But she must go to Grace's engagement party—alone—and capitalize on the opportunity to spread her own rumors about their ill-fated union. After all, she had told Jasper she would.

She had even told her friends and tried to ignore how genuinely disappointed they all appeared at such news. Especially when they were evidently trying so hard to ensure Elizabeth and Jasper truly did end up married.

A soft knock sounded at the door. Her maid entered with a small notecard. "It's from Lady Brightstone," she said hastily, as though she herself could feel that small kick of hope in Elizabeth's chest that the missive might be from Jasper.

Not that it mattered if it was or wasn't from him. After all, what could he say that would change her mind? She would not marry someone who could not love her.

She unfolded the note from Hannah.

Dearest Elizabeth,

I am sorry I cannot attend the ball due to my delicate condition—at least I'm finally considered delicate by some means. Ha! Best of luck this evening. I shall be thinking of you.

But that is not all, I'm including an invitation to Spinster's Sanctuary. They know to expect you whether it is tonight or any time this month.

All my love,

H

Spinster's Sanctuary— the affectionate name they had given to Rosewood Manor, the beautiful home Hannah's husband gifted her on their wedding as an escape for her, should she ever need it. The idea of the grand home had been part of their plan when they were all girls who decided to never marry, a refuge for them to congregate. And with Hannah being the first to marry, her husband had lovingly honored that dream with his generous present.

Elizabeth washed her face at the basin, the water ice cold and refreshing against the heat of her cheeks and eyes. The idea of getting away from London held great appeal to be sure. With that thought tucked nicely in the back of her mind, she hastily dressed and slipped into Grace's room to help her sister prepare for her own engagement party.

ELIZABETH COULDN'T TAKE her eyes off her sister, her chest swelling with pride.

Their father announced Grace's engagement officially and she and Scorbridge had been inseparable throughout the evening ever since. Whether they were swirling over the dance floor or engaged in conversation, their eyes were starry with affection for one another.

Jasper had looked at Elizabeth like that.

His stare had been convincing even though she'd known he was acting. Yet there were so many moments she still recalled so vividly, like how he'd held her upright when they danced, after she'd so boldly teased him toward intimacy.

And how later, he'd deliciously obliged in the shadowed alcove of their patio.

"Have you told people yet?" Amy's voice startled Elizabeth.

"I beg your pardon?" Elizabeth turned to her friend and found not only Amy, but also Lucy and Jillian staring at her expectantly.

"You don't have to say anything, you know," Lucy offered.

"He looked at you like that." Jillian nodded across the room to where Grace and Scorbridge gazed adoringly at one another.

"Any way he regarded me was part of the ruse," Elizabeth whispered.

"Was it?" Jillian arched a brow.

"Whose side are you on in all of this?" Elizabeth asked, incredulous.

"Always yours," Lucy said vehemently.

"Which is why we want to make sure you are certain this is really what you want," Amy said.

"Of course it is," Elizabeth replied.

The three exchanged a dubious look.

"Then you will likely have your chance." Jillian glanced toward Lady Hasselton as she approached, one of her ever-present feathers in her hair bobbing about behind her like an errant antenna.

Elizabeth steeled herself.

Lady Hasselton was keen on disproving the public love match between Jasper and Elizabeth for the scandal it was. There was a high likelihood she had been the source behind the scandal sheets finding out about Elizabeth being caught alone in the study with Jasper before Lady Gentry announced their surprise engagement. Lady Hasselton would certainly delight in hearing Elizabeth admit that she felt as though she and Jasper did not suit, and that she was strongly considering releasing him from his promise to marry her.

The countess paused in front of them, waving a fan in front of her face that set her feather bobbing at a frenzied pace. "I wager your father would be delighted if you have an engagement party soon," she said to Jillian.

"I'd sooner announce the opening of an art school than I would a proposal." Jillian smiled sweetly.

"Goodness, but you say the most preposterous things." Lady Hasselton scoffed and gave a little snort of laughter. "An art school indeed!" To Elizabeth, the older woman nodded. "Your mother is lucky to be marrying off two daughters in one season."

The moment was ideal for Elizabeth to share her unhappiness with Jasper, to lay the public fodder for an impending dismissal of their engagement.

Elizabeth opened her mouth.

Suddenly she wondered at Jasper reading the scandal sheets the following day, seeing their dissolution in bold print, detailed for all to see.

And would he be disappointed?

As disappointed as Elizabeth?

"Speaking of Lord Darington, he appears to be absent this evening." Lady Hasselton made a point of looking about with great exaggeration.

Her purposeful demeanor in noting Jasper's absence needled Elizabeth. "Mama is overjoyed at the prospect of two impending weddings," she said finally, intentionally ignoring the opportunity to confirm Jasper was not in attendance, that they were preparing to part ways with one another.

Lady Hasselton did not appear to be put off by the exclusion of information, likely because her busybody pestering was often ignored.

"That last sister of yours will be married by the end of the season," Lady Hasselton declared. "That's how it is with sisters when more than one marries in a season. The other always follows. You mark my words. Especially as she is the prettiest of you three."

She beamed as if she'd just bestowed the kindest of compliments, then swept away to join several friends, nearly hitting Lucy in the face with the feather. Lucy scowled unabashedly at the woman's retreating back.

"That was interesting," Jillian mused. "There was no mention of your fiancé."

Amy blinked and looked to Elizabeth "Why didn't you—?"

Elizabeth shook her head, eyes welling with unexpected tears. She didn't want to be here anymore, surrounded by people who were asking where Jasper was, knowing she ought to tell them she was unhappy with him, and being entirely aware that she could not.

"Hannah offered me the use of Spinster's Sanctuary," she said instead. "I think I am inclined to accept the opportunity. I need to think, to clear my head. Of him." Her voice caught and she indicated the room of people with couples dancing and flirting and staring into each other's eyes. "Of all this."

"When will you go?" Lucy asked, not seeming at all surprised by Elizabeth's announcement. Likely Hannah had told the others of her idea before making the offer to Elizabeth.

Now, Elizabeth thought mournfully. But sadly, now was not an option.

"I shall leave in the morning," she replied instead. "Once I've had my bags packed and can speak with Mama about taking one of the maids with me."

Amy smiled softly and rested a hand on Elizabeth's forearm. "I hope some time away helps."

Elizabeth nodded in appreciative agreement, hoping herself that the escape from London truly did help to free her heart from Jasper's grip.

JASPER TOOK his time reading during breakfast that morning. Elizabeth's ribbon remained curled around his hand as Hughes set about preparing him for the day, uncharacteristically quiet as if understanding Jasper's dark mood.

Once impeccably dressed and prepared for the day, Jasper did not leave the ribbon behind as he normally did, but left it curled in his pocket. A foolish attachment to remind him of the woman who had declined his offer of marriage. He reached for the door handle of his bedchamber and his hand shook, a sign of nerves he could not steady.

The scandal pages would be filled with Elizabeth's self-imposed gossip, spreading word of their ill-suited match.

Part of him was dreading reading those words, to know that whatever had begun to blossom between them was irreparably withering. And yet another part of him—a harder, calloused part—wanted to know the task was complete and be done with the whole business so he could bloody well move on with his life.

Business of the estates would always occupy his time, and he'd put far too much aside in his pursuit of Elizabeth. The time had returned to focus on the Fitzroy estates.

Bess was casually reading the gossip pages when he entered room. He had expected theatrics, tears. At the very least some soul-suffering sighs.

She elicited none.

"Anything of note in the paper?" He hedged.

She lowered the large page. "By paper, I assume you mean my scandal sheets?"

A footman settled a plate of toast points in front of him and Jasper gave a noncommittal hum in reply to Bess's question. As if his heart was not tethered to the words printed in that blasted newssheet. As if his anxiety was not rendering his nerves raw and ragged.

"There was news about Elizabeth's sister's engagement." Bess put a hand to her chest, her blue eyes sparkling. "Such a lovely couple. There were so many remarks about how happy they looked."

Jasper tensed, waiting for her to continue.

When she did not, he frowned. "Was nothing else mentioned?"

"Well, it was noted that you were not present." Bess tossed him a smirk. "You ought to have listened to me when I told you repeatedly you should be in attendance."

Good God, was Bess toying with him?

His jaw clenched. "And nothing else?"

Bess tilted her head in consideration. "There was rather a nice compliment on the floral arrangements." She lifted her brow. "Was there supposed to be more?" She sat up a little straighter. "There was a reason you didn't go last night, wasn't there? Jasper, what have you done?"

"We didn't think my attendance would be prudent when we knew we were intending to break the engagement."

"Break the engagement?" Bess wailed. "But there is still more time and you can still win her over."

But he was shaking his head. "You know I tried."

"Once." Bess put a finger in the air. "Sometimes women require more than one nudge to where they need to go. Your grandfather had to ask me three times, and the third I nearly said no."

"I've given up, Bess."

She shook her head. "Why didn't you tell me?"

"Because I knew you'd act exactly like this," he offered dryly.

She sprang to life and clutched a hand to her chest. "I'm dying. I'm going to die without great-grandchildren."

Jasper rolled his eyes.

Bess grasped the tablecloth, gasping as a footman rushed forward to catch a cup of tea before it could upend onto the carpet below.

Jasper reached for the newssheet and snapped it open. "If you're done dying, I shall tell you what transpired."

She snapped upright, her cheeks as rosy as a woman three decades her junior. Though she had asked several times what they'd spoken of at the picnic, Jasper had not shared. His heart had not been able to take the pain.

"Are you sure you won't expire if I speak plainly with you?" he asked, his tone droll. "I can't have you upsetting the footmen."

She waved him off as if he was a pesky fly. "No, no, perfectly fine."

"I asked her to marry me, and she asked if I loved her."

Bess's face fell, eyes sad, her dejected expression relaxing into soft, wrinkled skin. Suddenly she looked older than she had since he'd known her.

Her immediate understanding stung.

"Is it so obvious I can't love?" Jasper snapped, immediately regretted having done so.

His inability to love had nothing to do with Bess. In fact, any part of him capable of love was due to her.

His grandmother reached for him and set her hand on his forearm, her touch gentle. "The only thing I find obvious is that you think you cannot love. Your parents took advantage of your love for your brother, putting far too much trust in a boy to take on the responsibility of a parent." Bess frowned. "I shall never forgive my son for the pressure he put upon you, nor the blame he laid at your feet. But do not let them keep you from being with the woman you love."

"I don't love her," Jasper protested.

"Don't you?" Bess chuckled softly.

"Is this about how I look at her?" Jasper asked, vexed. He'd heard enough of all that. "Such things are easily feigned."

"You aren't one for feigning, Jasper." She smiled at him, her features relaxing with affection. "Besides, it is more than that, such as how you are always there to catch her if she stumbles and set her at ease. And how she stands up for you and looks up to you, like you hung the stars in the sky."

"She doesn't look up to me," Jasper protested. "She knows my reputation."

"This is why you think you aren't good enough for her?" Bess asked.

Ah, yes. Jasper recalled he had shared that bit with Bess, though he now regretted having done so. Already he felt far too exposed in this conversation.

"You are worthy of her, Jasper," Bess said firmly. "And she feels you are worthy of her too. If she did not, she wouldn't love you."

Jasper's brows lifted. "You think she loves me?"

Now Bess grinned, revealing her straight, small teeth. "I know she does. It's why she couldn't marry you unless you loved her—which you do. The girl is a smart one. No woman can risk her heart around you, Jasper, my boy."

"But I'm incapable of love," Jasper protested.

"Stuff and nonsense." Bess harrumphed. "If you were incapable of love, you wouldn't care that I'm dying."

"You're not dying."

She gave a good-natured laugh. "You wouldn't care that I want a great-grandchild or that I want to see you happily married." She took his hand in hers, her skin soft with age and cool to the touch. "Jasper, my boy, you are entirely capable of love, and you love that woman who absolutely loves you."

Jasper blinked and thought about Elizabeth and how much not having her in his life left a vast emptiness, how he anticipated seeing her and marveled at her candid responses, at the way she deeply saw him when everyone else seemed content to judge only the mask he presented. How he relished selecting flowers for her by hand, each bouquet inspired in some way by his sentiment toward her.

By God, he *was* in love.

And he *would* get her back.

He pushed up from the table abruptly.

Bess gave a little cry of surprise, then beamed. "There's a determined look about you that I rather like."

"Have the carriage readied posthaste," he informed the footman.

Bess clapped her hands, then clasped them excitedly before her bosom. "Are you going after Elizabeth?"

"I am," he declared. "And I won't stop until she is mine."

Because he was in love, damn it, and wouldn't waste another moment by not telling her.

15

"I'm sorry, but Lady Elizabeth is not at home." The butler repeated the phrase for the second time.

"Not in or not accepting callers?" Jasper asked, seeking confirmation.

The man's mouth pressed into a flat line, giving him the appearance of a turtle. "I am not at liberty to say, my lord."

"Will you tell her it's urgent that Lord Darington sees her. You have my card."

The butler nodded in agreement and held the card up, pinched between his forefingers as evidence.

Jasper took a step back and looked up at the upper levels of the townhouse, as if expecting Elizabeth to appear at one of the windows so that he might call to her like some woebegone Romeo. When she didn't, he had no choice but to leave, burdened with dejection.

The ride home left his mind churning, wondering how he could reach her. Likely through her friends, their addresses easily procured through a servant's inquiry.

Yes, that would be the ideal course of action.

Bolstered, he dashed up the steps to his townhouse and was met with the sound of tittering giggles.

What the devil?

He followed the sound into the drawing room where Bess was entertaining several young women, one of whom was immensely swollen with child, her red hair almost as bright as her spring-green gown. Lady Brightstone.

Just the woman he'd hoped to see.

In fact, every woman his grandmother was entertaining was one of Elizabeth's friends.

"I wonder…" He stepped toward the women, careful how he chose his words. "That is, I have to speak with Elizabeth, but her butler claims she is not at home. Would one of you be so kind as to pass on a message for me?"

"And why do you need to speak with her?" Miss Beauchamp asked, skepticism hard in her hazel eyes.

"Because he loves her." Bess clapped her hands like an overly excited child.

"Is that true?" Miss Honeyfield looked at him with such hope on her face that her affection for Elizabeth was irrefutable.

Jasper gave a solemn nod. "I never should have let things progress to this point. I ought to have been up front from the first, to let her know how I…"

He tapered off. His heart was not for them. It was for Elizabeth alone.

But apparently his speech had been enough for Lady Brightstone to give him a broad smile, her hand set atop her round belly. "We can do better than pass on a message. We know where she is so that you might deliver what you wish to say in person."

Jasper tilted his head. "Is she not in London?"

"I offered her the use of my private retreat," Lady Brightstone said proudly. "Knowing she would go there."

"And that if you wanted to find her," Miss Honeyfield added, "we could tell you exactly where to go."

"If you truly loved her and we knew your intentions to be true," Miss Beauchamp added, that warning glint still evident in her gaze.

At this point, Bess gave Jasper a knowing smile. "I assumed correctly that there was great benefit to acquainting myself with these clever young ladies."

"She left for Rosewood Manor this morning," Lady Jillian said. "Or as we call it, the Spinster's Sanctuary. It's located in Kent."

Spinster's Sanctuary?

But with the wistful look that touched Lady Jillian's face, he opted not to question the odd name.

The five women stared at him expectantly.

"I imagine if you leave now, you'll arrive not long after her." Lucy nodded encouragingly.

"And if I leave by horseback, I might arrive when she does," he mused aloud.

"Marvelous," Hannah exclaimed. "Oh, I haven't had this much fun in an age."

The women began chatting amongst themselves, but Jasper did not stay to listen. He exited the room with purposeful strides to seek out his valet to pack his satchel and his stable master to prepare his steed posthaste.

He needed to see Elizabeth, to proclaim his love.

Devil's Snare—or Devil, as Jasper affectionately referred to him—was waiting for him when he arrived at the stable, saddled and stocked with a bag of provisions. The black stallion nuzzled Jasper when he arrived, and immediately began nodding his great head with an urgency. Devil had a penchant for galloping when he ought to trot, and a determination that set him above the rest. He pawed the ground impatiently, his skin quivering with anticipation, even as Jasper secured his satchel and swung up into the waiting saddle.

Jasper needed only to click his tongue and his steed was off like a shot, charging through the mews, edging around London traffic with apparent aggravation. Paved streets gave way to hard-packed dirt roads, and finally Devil was stretching his legs out in a full gallop on the outskirts of the city.

Heavy clouds hung overhead, promising rain that Jasper hoped might leave off for long enough for him to arrive at Spinster's Manor, or whatever they'd called it.

The day was long, with Jasper scanning the horizon for Elizabeth's carriage, even as he paused from time to time to offer Devil a respite. Not that the young stallion needed one. Jasper had scarcely caught his own breath before the beast was pawing at the earth once more, eager to race across the countryside after being penned up in the city for far too long.

They were close to the area surrounding Spinster's Place when rain began to spit down at them from the heavy clouds.

Not that it mattered as they were very nearly there.

And then, of all ridiculous things, a tree stump came into view at the side of the road, not at all noticeable until they were directly upon it.

Devil's Snare had always been fearless, uncaring if a cape flapped in his periphery, heedless if someone shouted near his head, and impervious to rain or shine, sleet or snow. But good

God, how that horse detested tree stumps. As if these bits of foreign material jutted up from the earth with malintent, specifically to cause his demise.

Just as Jasper caught sight of the tree stump, Devil leapt from the earth as if it suddenly turned to flame, bucking his unease with a frantic, frenzied fear.

"It's only a stump, boy," Jasper soothed through gritted teeth as he tried desperately to hang on.

His foot slipped from one stirrup.

Jasper clung to the horse's broad body with the force of his inner thighs. But his efforts were no match for the next buck, which sent him flying from the massive horse, directly toward that stump.

An explosion of pain rang out at the back of Jasper's head as his body tumbled awkwardly to the ground. Stars danced in his eyes and mixed with the flecks of raindrops coming faster now, pelting his face with what felt like ice.

If only it could reach the back of his head where agony thundered in time with his heartbeat.

If only he wasn't so damnably tired and had the energy to move. If only he'd managed to arrive at Spinster's... cottage?

The world around him grayed out around the edges.

Of course his life would end like this, fading away as he finally found someone who loved him precisely for who he was. His only regret was not first seeing Elizabeth.

To tell her he loved her.

ELIZABETH SAT in the window seat of her bedchamber at

Spinster's Sanctuary, a book sitting in her lap like dead weight.

The exquisite manor contained a music room, an art room, and a well-appointed kitchen, should any of the women decide to try their hand at baking, as Amy had so often claimed to want to do. And, of course, a sprawling library, stacked with volumes of books.

There was no reason for Elizabeth's ennui. Especially when she had only arrived within the last hour, yet an entire day seemed to have passed in that short time she'd been there.

Her sigh puffed a cloud of fog on the window. She had come here to escape her woes, to be free of the burden of her troubles, and they had followed her, like specters, haunting her every thought.

Rain lashed at the windows, streaking the glass with rivulets that ran together, drawing her attention from the forgotten volume of *Sense and Sensibility* in her lap as her mind spun and spun and spun.

Movement in the yard caught her attention. A horse, black as pitch, its saddle empty as it trotted about in the front lawn of the manor house.

She sat upright, peering through the rain-streaked glass to better see. Yes, there was indeed a horse on the lawn absent its rider.

Had someone come to call and their horse jolted off without them?

But who would possibly be by to call?

Frowning, Elizabeth set aside her book and called for Susan, the maid her parents had spared to accompany her to Spinster's Sanctuary.

The young woman, a nervous, newly employed maid who

had a tendency to wring her fingers together and chatter on about her younger sister who she doted on, appeared immediately.

"Am I mad, or is there a riderless horse outside?" Elizabeth indicated the window.

"Mercy me." Susan put a hand to her chest. "I'll notify the butler immediately."

Elizabeth ran after her, desperate for a distraction from the prison of her mind and that endless churning of her thoughts. The butler immediately summoned a footman who ran out into the driving rain while the stable master was called.

Despite the awful weather, Elizabeth followed the footman outside and waited on the porch as he approached the black stallion. Even from a distance, Elizabeth could tell it was a fine animal, the muscles strong beneath the glossy, wet coat. This was a gentleman's horse to be sure.

But what gentleman would be out in this area when the London season was on?

Her heart caught, especially as she recalled having been told of a certain horse who was beautiful and powerful and all black.

No. She would not allow herself to accept that the rider might be Jasper. While their engagement had not yet been formally called off, it was as good as done. They had said their piece, and there was nothing for it.

He would not have come to her.

And yet...

A breath caught in her throat as the horse continued to dart away from the footman, rushing toward the gate leading to the main road. As if trying to encourage the man to follow him.

"I think he wants you to follow," Elizabeth called, her breath forming little clouds in the damp, icy air.

The man could not hear and jogged closer to Elizabeth. "I beg your pardon, my lady?"

The horse immediately followed the footman as though trying to reclaim the man's attention.

"He wants you to follow," Elizabeth tried again.

Panic curled around her heart, catching it in an iron grip.

Because what if it was Jasper's horse? What if this was Devil's Snare, whom he'd spoken of with such pride?

And why would Jasper no longer be on him?

Propriety be damned, she ran out into the rain, ignoring the stinging pelt of the frigid droplet and the footman's pleas to return to the manor. Up close, she saw a scar on the horse's chest, a mark made by the trainer who had so cruelly tried to whip the horse into submission.

The breath choked from her. This absolutely was Devil's Snare.

"Lord Darington was riding this horse," she called to the footman. "He is in need of assistance. Ready the carriage."

The footman ran off to do as he was bidden, shouting to the stable master who was rapidly approaching.

Devil's Snare nuzzled Elizabeth in an anxious bid to gain her attention.

"You have my full attention," she promised, turning the palm of her hand to his soft muzzle. "Take us to your master and I shall pray it is not too late."

Then, without thought, she came round the side of the

horse, lifted her skirts to affix her left foot into the stirrup, then gripped the saddle and swung herself up into the seat.

She scarcely had time to readjust the reins before the horse was off at a canter, rushing toward the gate. She turned him toward the stables and he aggressively turned back to the gate.

The stable master followed behind her, a single horse affixed to a simple wooden wagon. "This will do in a pinch," he called.

Elizabeth allowed Devil's Snare to race onward, pausing to slow the gallop to a trot, to ensure the carriage could keep up. On the open road, there was no slowing the beast as he raced down the path.

He stopped abruptly, pacing backwards with apparent unease. That's when Elizabeth saw him.

Jasper.

Lying perfectly still beside a tree stump nestled in the grass along the side of the road.

She swung her leg over the saddle, hopping down into the mud and ran to him, falling beside where he lay.

"Jasper," she cried, her voice a shriek amid the roar of driving rain.

He did not acknowledge her and fear gripped her hear.

He was so still. Too still.

No. This couldn't be.

He had come all the way here. For her.

By God, she would not lose him now.

She grabbed the lapels of his jacket and screamed his name. His brow flinched and she gasped out a sob.

He wasn't dead.

Thank God.

She caught his hand. "We'll get you help."

The stable master appeared.

"He's alive, but needs a physician," she said, unable to pull her gaze from Jasper's face, which had once again fallen still.

"I'll get him on the wagon, my lady, and we'll summon the physician."

"Take Devil's Snare to the physician." Elizabeth relinquished her hold on Jasper and pushed to her feet. "I'll drive the wagon."

The stable master drew up. "My lady, I cannot let you—"

"You can." She bent to help lift Jasper. "His life is more important than anything else."

He did not protest as she helped him carry Jasper's limp form to the bed of the wagon, a reassuring groan emanating from somewhere in Jasper's throat.

Good. If he was groaning, he was alive.

There was still a chance he wouldn't...

No. She refused to even think of that horrible outcome.

It was too impossible to imagine his strength, his vitality, the caring affection of his person, snuffed out forever.

The stable master drew up into Devil's Snare's saddle and the two of them were off as Elizabeth sat on the plank seat and took the reins of the mare, careful to drive quickly while also keeping the wagon as steady as possible.

Back at the manor, the footman from earlier rushed out to meet her, his hair still damp and his uniform limp from having been drenched once before by the rain. Together with the butler, they carried Jasper into the manor, only this time he did not move or groan, his face impossibly pale.

He was settled on the bed in one of the many rooms, and there was nothing for it but to wait for the physician.

The abrupt end of activity was Elizabeth's undoing.

Without her hands busy, her thoughts were wont to trail to places she did not want them to wander.

Thoughts of what could happen if the doctor was delayed, if he did not arrive in time. If there was nothing he could do.

Elizabeth had accepted weeks ago that she was in love with Jasper. What she had not allowed herself to realize was that he also loved her.

Though he said he did not, his love was evident—in the number of times he caught her as she tripped, in his nonchalant ease at helping her, and in his lack of chastisement for her clumsiness. And even in the times he himself had taken the attention to spare her, like when he spilled the sauce on his cravat.

She had been a fool to think he did not love her. And there was surely a reason for his hesitation to accept that he did. Likely the same reason that drew him towards the arms of many lovers during his grand tour.

The tears came faster, hot where they tracked down her cheeks as she clasped his hand and silently prayed for the physician to hurry.

She could not lose him, not when she only just realized she truly had him...and he had her.

16

*L*ight winked in and out of Jasper's consciousness amid gentle, soothing touches that graced his brow.

A man's authoritative voice mixed with a soft, familiar one that made Jasper's chest ache worse than his head.

Elizabeth.

He needed to tell her...His thoughts fractured and he frowned, his eyes closed against his sensitivity to the light.

He needed to tell her...

That he loved her.

He squinted his eyes open, his resolve strengthening as he fought the shards of pain splintering in his brain.

He needed to tell her he loved her, damn it.

"Elizabeth," he groaned aloud.

A cool hand folded around his. "I'm here."

He blinked his eyes fully open, fixing his attention on the beautiful face coming into focus before him. Her broad forehead and high cheekbones, a lush mouth with a full lower lip that brought back memories he loved to savor, and those wide blue eyes that captured his soul. Her hair was down, a riot of waves that appeared to be somewhat damp.

"Elizabeth," he said softly.

She smiled at him. "I'm here," she repeated.

"I love you." He gripped her hand, as if he could convey the depth of his feelings with his grasp on her. "I love you."

Her eyes sparkled. "I know."

His brow furrowed in thought as he combed through his mind to recall when he might have told her. "Did I…had I told you already?"

She shook her head. "I already knew. I thought back on the way you never cared what others thought when I tripped, or how you intentionally pulled the focus of others off me to spare my feelings when I spilled or did something clumsy. I thought about how you made it a point to spend time with me every day before we even decided that being publicly visible together would be more convincing. And in the time we spent together, I could tell you enjoyed our conversations as much as I did." Her teeth sank shyly against that full bottom lip he loved so much. "And there are other ways in which we appear rather compatible…"

He knew exactly what she implied with such a statement, and he grinned.

"Was that why you came here?" she asked. "To tell me?"

Here?

Where the devil was he?

For the first time since he'd woken, he looked about at his surroundings. The room was awash in delicate sea-foam green, the furniture carved with flowers and vines with accents of gilded petals.

A woman's room.

"Did I make it to Spinster's Space?" He sat up slightly and the room spun. "Is this your bedchamber?"

Wincing, he lowered himself back down on the bed.

Elizabeth reached for him, gently guiding him back to the plump pillow behind his neck. A sigh escaped him as he sank into it once more, allowing the softness to cradle the weight of his aching head.

"Spinster's Sanctuary," she corrected with a laugh. "And you did not make it entirely." Her mirth faded as her expression sobered. "Devil's Snare appeared in the yard and took me directly to where you had fallen and hit your head."

Ah, that explained the pain radiating from the base of his skull. "A tree stump?" he deduced.

"You remember?" she asked.

He smirked. "No, but it is the only thing Devil is afraid of." He placed his palm at his brow. "How long have I been here?"

"Only an hour," Elizabeth soothed. "The doctor just left and said you will need rest for a few days."

A few days?

He would need to notify Bess, to let his secretary know to manage the estates without him.

"I've already sent word to your grandmother to let her know," Elizabeth said, as though reading his thoughts.

Jasper relaxed. The estate would be in good hands with Bess. In fact, it might be in better order when he returned back to London. The woman knew how to run things in perfect order.

"If I wasn't so certain Bess would never do anything to hurt me, I'd assume she put that tree stump in my path to ensure I remained here for several days." He chuckled, imagining just how far Bess might go otherwise to secure his match with Elizabeth. His happiness.

"You may stay as long as you need." Elizabeth held his hand.

She remained thus, at his side, her small hand curled around his, keeping him company until he fell asleep. When he awoke again, he found her quietly reading one of the volumes of *Sense and Sensibility* he'd purchased for her, and she read to him until he drifted into slumber once more. Every time he woke, she was still there, meeting his sleepy gaze with a smile and asking after what he might have need of.

"No one has ever been so attentive toward me before," he said as she handed him a fresh cup of tea, steeped just a minute longer than necessary, exactly how he liked. "My grandmother tried, but I think at that point, I was much older and not inclined to be coddled."

"Why is that?" Elizabeth asked in that frank way of hers.

He held the teacup in his hand, letting its heat sink into his palms. "I think I was too angry, which I'm sure you'll ask me about next."

Elizabeth tilted her head in agreement. "I'd wager this had something to do with your life before you left for your grand tour. You brushed off my question about it when we took the carriage ride in Hyde Park, and I didn't want to pry..."

"But you're curious," he supplemented for her.

"I want to know you." She put her hand on his forearm, her touch delicate, yet strongly supportive. "I relish all the stories you've told me so I can understand you better, to know you more fully."

"You may not like what you learn," he cautioned cynically.

Elizabeth merely smiled. "You haven't put me off thus far."

No one had wanted to know him before. Not his parents, who saw him only as a means to care for his brother and provide a spare son for the title. Not the women he entertained throughout Europe on his grand tour, who wanted him only for what he could provide over the course of several nights. Not even his friends, who accepted the casual humor of his replies and declined to delve deeper—not that he'd have indulged their queries.

"I've never talked about what happened with Benjamin," he admitted, feeling rather foolish.

"You can talk about it with me."

And he knew in that moment that he absolutely could. "Benjamin was older than me by a year. You wouldn't know it to look at us when we were boys. He was shorter than me, his frame slight, his pallor sickly. My parents placed the world on those narrow shoulders, but they were never strong enough to support their dreams for him. Nonetheless, he was always the sole recipient of their love and affection. I was the second son, the spare, the one who was named after another second son who never ascended to the earldom because of my father's robust health."

There was a tinge of anger in his words as he spoke, a bitterness staining those memories.

"I was charged with protecting my brother," he continued. "That was my lot in life, to protect Benjamin so my secondary role as being the spare son would never have to be realized." He swallowed. "And I failed."

"I doubt that," Elizabeth countered.

"I did though." He closed his eyes, and he remembered the chill of the water gliding against his skin as he swam out, deeper and deeper into the lake, knowing Benjamin could never swim that far. "We had an argument one day when Benjamin didn't want me following him. I told him I hated following him. I hated how I was charged with minding him like a nanny. I was eight, he was nine, and I resented how much of my life was focused on him, just as he resented my constant shadow. He told me to leave him alone, that he never wanted a younger brother. I know he said it in the heat of the moment, but his words stung nonetheless. Angry and hurt, I turned away and rushed off to the lake. I'd always wanted to swim to the middle, to clear my thoughts, but was never allowed because he could not swim that far. I heard him calling behind me." An unexpected knot formed in Jasper's throat, callused by years of ignoring the pain that never stopped burning in his chest.

"I knew he was calling me and I still left, diving into the water." Jasper looked at the cup of tea, now cold in his hands. "I didn't hear him dive in after me, likely to apologize. That was kind of the person he was, someone who would make right the wrongs he'd done." His voice caught and he shook his head, momentarily overwhelmed by his swelling sorrow.

"He drowned that day when he tried to come after me." Japer hung his head. "I killed him."

"No." Elizabeth took the cold cup from his hands and shook her head vehemently. "No, you did not."

"He never would have gone out to the lake if I—"

"You never should have been charged with watching him," Elizabeth said gently. "If he was so ill, he ought to have had someone at his side, a nurse who could care for him. You didn't know he was swimming after you."

"My parents didn't believe that." Jasper let himself be

swept into the determination in her eyes, taking comfort in the way they captivated him with her sincerity. "My mother was never the same after Benjamin died. She stayed in her room, wearing her nightdress, not caring for herself. She died within a year, and my father claimed it was from a broken heart. Because of what I had done."

Elizabeth was already shaking her head.

"I spent the remainder of my youth in anger before graduating from Eton and going on for my grand tour," Jasper continued. "I lost myself in distractions without a care for the future or how others might perceive me. While I was gone, my father passed away as well." He shrugged. "And then it was just Bess and I."

"And I'm assuming your grandmother will agree with me that what happened to Benjamin was not your fault."

He nodded. "She is greatly displeased with how my father —her son—treated me. Of my entire family, she is the only one who has ever truly cared for me, who has seen me as who I am and accepted me as that. Until you..."

"I've seen you for who you are since that night in the study at Lady Gentry's ball." She gave a wistful smile, as if she was remembering. "And I've always been keen to know more about you. I'm honored you've shared as much as you have with me, that you've trusted me."

He reached for her, unable to think of anyone he would rather trust than her.

"I love you, Elizabeth," he said softly. Deeply. Truly.

And if she answered him back, he did not hear as he faded into slumber once more, his heart lighter than it had been in years.

Elizabeth stayed at Jasper's side as he slept, taking her meals there and having his at the ready when he woke.

In the first hour after he'd initially come to, his need to squint his eyes against the light had relaxed and his thoughts seemed clearer, more coherent. Even the periods of sleep he fell into appeared to happen less and less.

"It's getting late," Jasper said, his voice gravelly from sleep.

"Not so late." Elizabeth knew the time to be somewhere just past eleven at night. Late enough that she had encouraged the staff to seek out their own beds, assuring them she would be fine to see to herself and Jasper. "I've read far later into the evening than this."

He grinned at her, that lopsided, boyish way of his that pulled at her heart. "You don't intend to stay at my bedside all night, do you?"

She considered his words. "I might."

"The bed is far more comfortable." He scooted over, making space for her on the broad mattress. Indeed, there was plenty of room.

It would be a terrible lack of propriety to join him.

But then, they'd had no one in the room with them to protect her virtue. Or be a witness to such scandalous behavior either. After all, the staff knew that Elizabeth and Jasper were engaged, and regardless, any good employee did not share secrets.

An ache of discomfort had begun to burn at the back of Elizabeth's spine, and the hard seat of the wooden chair was digging into her backside. The idea of lying down on the bed was indeed appealing.

The idea of doing so in Jasper's arms was entirely irresistible.

Without letting herself question what she was doing, she slid off the chair and onto the mattress beside him, lying atop the covers as he rested beneath. Surely that was innocent enough, was it not?

He reached an arm around her shoulders and pulled her toward him so her head rested on the solid heat of his chest. His scent surrounded her, that sensual spice that made her blood go hot. Beneath the thin linen of his shirt, his heartbeat pounded deep and even against her cheek.

She had never been so close to a man before and was altogether entranced by the proximity. For this was not just any man, this was Jasper. The gentleman who had caught her attention the first time she saw him at the exact ball he'd first seen her, the gentleman who she had lied to her friends about having affection for, as she was certain he would want nothing to do with her.

"You're right, this is far more comfortable," she agreed, her words coming out like a purr.

His voice rumbled under her cheek as he replied, "I must truly have been concussed to have not thought of it before now." His chuckle jostled her slightly.

"I'm glad you came here," she admitted. "That we have this time to truly talk."

Jasper's hand stroked over her hair, likely still wild and loose from when she'd run out into the storm earlier. There was a quiet intimacy to allowing him to see her like this, a feeling she found she liked.

"When I told you I didn't know if I could love, I hadn't

meant because of you," Jasper said. "I meant in general. My parents accusations…they wounded me."

"I understand that now." Elizabeth scrunched her face with what she planned to confess, grateful she did not have to look at him as she spoke. "I never thought myself good enough for you, so when you said that…"

Jasper pulled back and looked down at her with incredulity. "I beg your pardon?"

She shrugged. "You have such an ease about you, always knowing exactly the right thing to say at the right moment. And you're very sure-footed." She gave a self-deprecating chuckle.

"I've learned to say the right thing to please people, to stay out from underfoot," he admitted. "But I have never once thought myself too good for you. Quite the contrary. I thought a woman as kind and thoughtful, as beautiful and reputable as you, was far too good for the likes of me. Especially with the stain of my reputation."

Her cheeks burned with the compliment, and she buried her face in his chest. "So much flattery."

"So much truth."

She looked up at him. "Perhaps we are just right for one another then, after all."

He did not lower his head and kept staring at her, his dark eyes lit with a desire she now understood, as it was the same desire kindling in her own blood. "I've always noticed you," he said. "I've always watched you, longed for you from afar."

"I don't believe you." She laughed as she said it, her cheeks growing hot.

He shifted on the bed, putting his hand under the coverlets. When it emerged, there was a white silk ribbon curled in his hands. One that looked very like what she tied her stockings up with.

"Is that…?"

"Your ribbon that came loose from your stocking that night," he confirmed.

She craned her neck up at him in surprise. "You truly kept it?"

"I've wanted you for so long, Elizabeth," he whispered. "You're beautiful, graceful—"

"Graceful?" She laughed at that.

He chuckled, a low, sensual timbre she felt in the marrow of her bones. "One of my first impressions of you was how graceful you were."

She raised her brows at him, skeptical. "I don't hear that often."

"You move like a dancer, all slender limbs…" He ran his fingertips over her arm, and shivers followed in the wake of his touch. "And your long, delicate neck." His touch grazed up her throat to rest at her chin. "And the most beautiful face I've ever seen."

Her cheeks burned with the sincere praise, and she merely lifted her shoulders in shy acknowledgment of his words.

"I've wanted you since I first saw you," he repeated in a low voice. "But you were as out of my grasp as an angel in the heavens."

"Until now," she said in a coy tone.

The corner of his mouth tucked upward. "Until now." He swallowed. "Do you recall that time at Lady Gentry's ball last season when you spilled lemonade on me?"

Mortified, she leaned her head back. "How could I forget?"

"You were so diligent in trying to mop up the mess, you

weren't paying attention to where your hands were going," he continued.

She groaned in humiliation.

"Your touch was accidental, but still you inadvertently stroked your hand over…" His voice was almost a whisper in the silent room and tapered off rather than say precisely the part of his body he referred to. "It was an innocent touch, but it burned me all the same. I thought about you every night since. Wondering if it had just been the two of us, how you might have helped me out of my clothes. How I might have helped you out of yours. How I might make you moan in pleasure. The way you did the night of our engagement party." His gaze wandered toward her mouth and lifted up once more to meet her eyes. "The way you sounded when your body released was even more exquisite than I had dared to imagine."

Her nipples tingled against her stays, that low pulse thrumming to life once more, warm between her legs where her body recalled the feel of his skilled fingers all too well.

"I never knew a touch could feel like that," she confessed. "I…have thought of it often. Of you often."

"Every night, I hope," he said. "The way I think of you."

She nodded and licked her lips, and his gaze dipped to her mouth once more.

He reached for her, and she stretched up the length of his body so their mouths met. He kissed as he had done before, his mouth moving over hers, his tongue teasing against her own.

This time, she was bold as she kissed him back, exactly as she had imagined being if she should have the chance again. She wanted to explore all of him, to savor his mouth, his touch, and to let her hands roam over his body as his had done with hers. To bring him pleasure as he had given so selflessly to her.

Jasper groaned as she kissed him back with fervor, deeper and hungrier than the groans he'd weakly emitted earlier when she found him outside by the tree stump.

At that thought, she pulled back abruptly. "Jasper, your head. We shouldn't…"

"We absolutely should," he growled, and pulled her against him. A hardness pressed against her hip, evidence of his desire for her. She melted against him, her protests dying on her lips, being kissed away so they were nothing more than a distant memory.

"I want you, Elizabeth." He spoke against her neck, amid a string of kisses that left desire prickling on her skin and shivering deliciously down her spine.

And God, did she want him in return.

17

Whatever ache had throbbed at the back of Jasper's skull was nothing more than a distant memory. He was far more interested in quelling a different throb now, one decidedly lower than his head. One now pressed against the softness of Elizabeth's body as she rocked against him with an innocent's frustrated longing.

How he wanted to strip her down and take her, plunge deep within her and make her his.

Except she was a virgin.

And not his wife.

She hadn't even said she loved him in return.

If he could think properly, that might have bothered him. But her mouth was sliding down his throat as he'd done with her, nipping at the skin as she raked her hands down his linen shirt so her fingernails grazed the skin beneath.

Good God, this woman was his undoing.

He pulled at the ties of her dress, loosening the bodice and lowering it to reveal the firm roundness of her breasts, each topped with a pink nipple going firm in the cool air. With a groan, he closed his mouth over one, flicking his tongue against the bud before biting it ever so gently.

Elizabeth cried out as she had before, her hands moving to the back of his head before quickly releasing him.

"I'm fine," he growled against her silken flesh.

"I don't want to hurt you," she gasped out.

"Nothing hurts right now," he assured her.

Still, he released her breasts and rolled her over onto her back, escaping the covers as he did so, freeing himself for everything he wanted to do her. For now wasn't just for touching, now was also for tasting.

Bracing his body over hers, he pulled at the skirt of her dress, easing it up her legs to reveal her mud-stained stockings, and the silk ties securing them just over her knees. He bent over her, gripping the first with his teeth and pulling it free.

She gave a gasp of surprise.

The first of what he hoped would be many.

He liberated the other ribbon and pulled the stockings down, revealing her shapely calves before tracing his way back up her legs once more, fingertips teasing flesh he intended for his mouth to sample.

Elizabeth closed her eyes and leaned her head back. That's when he bent forward, replacing his hands with his lips, kissing the sensual skin of her inner thighs.

"Jasper," she gasped.

Before she could have a thought toward modesty, his mouth closed over her sex, his tongue gliding up her center, tracing the slit toward the swollen bud to circle with the tip of his tongue.

Something between a gasp and a moan escaped her, and all

thoughts of modesty ceased as her legs eased open wider in silent permission for him to continue to please her with his mouth, his tongue.

She writhed beneath his attentions, her breath coming in panting cries. He swept his fingers against her entrance and she arched toward him. Tenderly, he continued to tease her with his tongue, tasting her arousal as his finger eased inside her. Once she became accustomed to the sensation of his finger, he thrust within her, loving her with the digit the way his body burned to do with his cock.

It would be so easy. She was so damn ready. So wet. So swollen with need.

Her thighs clenched and she turned to bury her face into the pillow next to her, the moans of her release muted by the thick down feathers as her sex clenched around his finger. He lapped at her a few more times, relishing the sensual allure of her until her hips bucked with sensitivity.

He grinned and pushed up on his elbow to gaze at the woman he loved, her wavy hair mussed, blue eyes bright with desire, her cheeks and lips flushed pink, breasts bared over the top of her bodice.

Good God, he'd never seen a woman more beautiful in his entire life.

Desire thundered through him, pulsing in his loins with a need stronger than any he'd ever known.

He lowered her skirts and crawled up the bed to join her, drawing her into his arms.

She leaned back, pulling away from him to look up at him. "Surely that is not all."

"I beg your pardon?"

"Don't play coy with me, Jasper Fitzroy." She lifted her

chin defiantly. "There is more to what happens between a man and a woman."

"When they are wed."

She smirked. "Not always."

His jaw dropped in shock and she laughed. "I told you rumors were scandalous things. I know far more than you think I do." She nudged him in the ribs.

Then the look in her eyes shifted, the glint of playfulness slitted to a sensuality that made him burn.

"I want to touch you as you've touched me." Her hands slid down his chest, his abdomen, to…to where she'd once tried to clean lemonade from the placket of his breeches before.

His cock lurched at the invitation of her warm hands, but he pulled his hips back. "You're innocent, Elizabeth. I won't ruin your reputation."

"I would not call what was just done *innocent*." A smile hovered at the corners of her lips. "Though I certainly enjoyed it."

"Our engagement is to be broken." He lifted a brow. "Is it not?"

She bit her lower lip and dragged her hands toward his stomach once more, then walked her fingertips lower to the edge of his breeches. "You haven't asked me to marry you again."

He swallowed, trying to remain focused. The woman was driving him to distraction in the best way possible.

"Will you marry me?" he asked, his voice husky.

She searched his gaze. "Do you love me?"

"I love you," he breathed. "With everything that I am, I love you."

She pressed her forehead to his. "And I love you," she whispered against his lips. "I think I've always loved you. From when we first met, and certainly from the moment you saved me in the study by agreeing that you were my fiancé. I fell deeper in love when you spilled gravy on your cravat so no one would notice me. And finally, I fell irrevocably head over heels when you trusted me by telling me why you feared love."

He kissed her then, without reservation, without holding back or giving a thought to her virginal state or his sordid reputation. They were a man and woman in love, a man and woman on the cusp of getting married.

And he had no intention of ever withholding anything from her ever again.

ELIZABETH YIELDED to the passion blazing within her, kissing her soon-to-be husband back with all the love and desire coursing through her. As his mouth captured hers and then moved down the sensitive line down her neck, her hands played over his clothing, following the landscape of rigid muscle and arousal beneath the layers of cloth.

"I want you," he growled against her skin, and she moaned in rely.

"Let me touch you." Her words were breathy with lust, with eagerness.

He sat up, grabbed the back of his shirt, and unceremoniously ripped it over the top of his head, leaving his dark hair messy and his chest rising and falling with the frenzy of his breath.

Elizabeth sat up, letting her gaze roam appreciatively over the beauty of his body, the hard lines of carved flesh, hollowing shadows across his torso where the firelight didn't touch. She ran her fingers across his soft, warm skin.

His eyes closed with pleasure, and he gave a little hum of approval as she stroked and explored his firm body with her fingertips, tentative at first, and then more boldly. Over the strength of his arms, down his powerful back, across the hard chest she'd laid her head upon, and down the valley of chiseled flesh to where his placket was fastened. A column strained against his breeches.

Her breath caught, knowing full well what that was, her heart hammering in anticipation. He leaned back on his elbows, gazing down at her where she kneeled next to him on the mattress, letting her decide how far she wished to go.

There would be no going back from this moment. And she had no intention of stopping.

She popped one of the buttons free. Then another. The placket shifted upward an inch. She lifted her brows, impressed, and he chuckled, the sound deep and throaty in a way that made her blood burn hotter.

The next two buttons almost sprang free on their own, releasing Jasper's phallus which rose in a hard column from a thatch of dark hair, pulsing to a beat that matched the one between her legs. Looking cautiously up at him, she stroked her fingers up from the base to the tip.

Jasper sucked in a hard inhale.

Emboldened by his reaction, she curled her fingers around the shaft, his skin like fiery silk against her palm. His hand closed over hers, guiding her to move over his hard member, up and down.

His breath became labored, his powerful chest flexing with each stroke of her hand.

A sense of power washed over her, to know that she could give him the same kind of pleasure he had given her, even with her lack of experience.

"I have to have you," he groaned. "If you keep going as you are, you'll unman me before I can take you."

"I want to please you," she protested.

He exhaled a laugh. "You have, more than you know." He sat up, pulling his breeches off, revealing strong legs dusted with dark hair, fully naked.

His voice was soft as he reached for the lacings of her bodice. "I want to see all of you too."

She knelt on the bed in front of him, watching him as he pulled the ribbon free, as the silk gown was drawn down, followed by her chemise. His eyes roamed over her with appreciation, his jaw clenching as if restraining himself. When her clothes were pooled around her knees, he eased her to her back and slid away the garments, leaving her naked.

He stretched his body over hers, the silky head of his phallus nudging eagerly against her despite the slow progression of his kisses.

Elizabeth widened her legs to cradle his body and arched toward him. "I want you, Jasper."

He paused, his expression furrowed. "I don't want to hurt you. I have heard from others that the first time can bring pain."

"Then be done with it, so there is no pain the next time." She smiled coquettishly up at him.

"You minx." He grinned down at her and eased slightly lower so the head of his sex pressed at her entrance.

Need roared through Elizabeth's body. She moaned and pushed up to meet him.

He eased in slowly and a slight discomfort pressed around her pleasure.

"I'm sorry, my love." His hips jerked, thrusting into her.

Pain cut through the haze of her desire, stark and intrusive.

But she knew from what she'd been told by others that the hurt was fleeting.

He bent to kiss her, holding his body in place as her body adjusted to the foreign feel of him inside her. Slowly, carefully, he began to move. Almost imperceptibly at first and then a gentle glide.

As he did this, his mouth moved over her collarbone, her neck, to the place behind her ear that made her skin prickle with goosebumps. And then, the pain began to yield to pleasure.

He was moving in her with a rhythm now, one she easily caught and matched with the rocking of her own hips, her breath once more becoming quick, catching on eager moans.

His movements began to slow, but she gripped his hips with her legs, trying to pull him against her more swiftly.

Then his hand was between their bodies, finding that glorious spot that made every part of her sing. A swirl of pleasure paired with the undulation of their bodies as they met again and again and again until she could stand it no longer.

Her body tightened with the now familiar sensation that preceded a release.

"Yes," Jasper growled, his hips moving faster now, their bodies joining with a frenzy that shoved her over the edge as her world splintered apart.

He bent his head to her neck, groaning against her skin as his hips flexed against her in a jerking rhythm that he likely could not control any more than she could stop the clenching of her sex around him.

They remained locked together thus for some time, as the slamming beat of their hearts calmed to a slow, steady thud and Elizabeth's limbs slackened with a sensual, languid tranquility of utter fulfillment.

Jasper rested his forehead against hers. "Now, when shall we get married?"

"Already?" She laughed.

He rolled off her and quirked an eyebrow. "And here I thought you read numerous novels."

She laughed again, feeling happier, and more satisfied than she ever knew possible. "Of course I have. What kind of question is that?"

"You know how it is with lovers." He lifted a shoulder. "If we wait too long to wed, I will meet some untimely demise and you will be left a young woman who never married, yet in a delicate way with my child."

Elizabeth appraised this man who had stolen her heart and loved her in the best ways. "Perhaps you read more novels than I do."

"Perhaps we shall discuss them together when we are man and wife."

She beamed up at him. "I should love nothing better."

"Nothing?" He skimmed a palm over her shoulder. Her skin warmed in response, her blood heating once more.

"Perhaps there are many pleasures to be shared together," she breathed.

"And we shall enjoy them all, dearest."

18

Jasper had once wondered how far Bess might go to see him married. Apparently, she would drop everything in London and race to his side in less than a day to arrive in time for an impromptu wedding in the country. Ironically, at an estate presumably created for spinsters.

Not that the wedding was entirely impromptu.

A second carriage followed behind hers, one laden with tulips and pastry confections, and a gown befitting the grandmother of the groom.

Jasper had been in the library, finishing the second volume of *Sense and Sensibility* in the large chair opposite to Elizabeth's before the fire, as she read the third volume.

"Forgive me, my lord," the butler interrupted. "But it appears the dowager Lady Darington has arrived."

A maid snuck a grin at the butler as he passed. The entire staff of Spinster's Something-or-other knew about the tryst Jasper and Elizabeth had been enjoying.

Elizabeth closed her book as did Jasper. "I imagine my mother and sisters will be following soon."

Jasper offered her his arm and together they hurried to the front door to greet Bess. "Shall we put a wager on who will arrive first—your mother and sisters, or your friends?"

Elizabeth laughed, an open, carefree sound he looked forward to hearing for the rest of his life. "I imagine they will be arriving close to one another."

Together, they pushed through the door just as Bess's carriage came to a stop, as did the one behind her.

The door to the coach flew open, knocking the footman back several steps as Bess erupted from it as though she'd never needed a walking stick in her life. She all but ran to Jasper, arms outstretched.

"My boy is getting married." Her eyes were bright, sparkling with unmitigated joy. "To a woman he loves." She pulled Elizabeth into an embrace. "It will be such a joy to have you in the family, my darling Elizabeth. Thank you for taking care of Jasper when he—"

Bess's mouth formed an 'o' and she wheeled around to Jasper once more. "Your head. Are you fully recovered?"

Jasper chuckled at her excitement and nodded. "I've had an attentive nurse."

Elizabeth's cheeks flamed red as she no doubt recalled precisely how she had nursed him back to fair health. Again and again and again.

"I'm so glad." Bess squeezed Elizabeth's arm. "Thank you for caring for him. I hope he wasn't too surly a patient."

Elizabeth tempered a grin, her face straining to remain sober as she spoke. "Not at all."

"Oh, and Jasper, I had the flowers we had ordered swapped

out for tulips." Bess beamed at Elizabeth. "He told me those are your favorite."

"I heard you've had quite the hand to play in all the flowers I've received," Elizabeth said with a genial smile.

Bess blinked. "Me? Oh, no, dear. Jasper went to the florist every morning before breakfast to hand-select each bouquet for you."

Jasper looked away, feigning innocence.

Elizabeth put her hands on her hips, playful in her chastisement. "You told me Bess had ordered all the flowers."

Bess gave a cackle. "This boy has been mooning over you since the moment I saw the two of you together. I'm just glad the two of you have finally realized how right you are for one another."

The rattle of a carriage pulled their attention to the gate once more as not one, but four carriages rolled up.

If Jasper and Elizabeth had indeed wagered on Elizabeth's friends or family arriving first, they would both have won as all those who loved Elizabeth poured from the open carriages, including Lord and Lady Brightstone, the latter holding her large stomach.

Jasper didn't bother to ask if travel was good for a woman so far along that she ought to be in confinement. He knew well enough she would absolutely not miss Elizabeth's wedding.

Both Jasper and Elizabeth were swallowed up by the delighted squeals of her family and friends. But before Jasper was pulled away, Bess reached out and clasped his shoulder. "I'm proud of you, my boy."

Then, without bothering to ask if he wanted it or not, she drew him into a hearty embrace and his heart swelled in his chest. His grandmother had always been his staunchest supporter and only true family. It gave him pleasure to know her joy at his impending marriage to a woman he loved.

And truly he did love Elizabeth, a woman who accepted him exactly as he was, who had convinced him to lower the barrier around his heart, to make himself vulnerable.

Beyond his reputation, beyond his past, beyond those who made him feel unworthy of love, unwanted. He knew now that none of it was true.

Elizabeth made him feel entirely loved. Absolutely wanted. And worthy of her in every regard.

There could not be a happier man more smitten with his wife in all of Christendom than Jasper was with his soon-to-be-wife.

A BRIDE never had so many women crowding around her as did Elizabeth the following morning. Ribbons were pulled here and there, a flower was adjusted in her hair, her skirts were fanned out and brushed over repeatedly. The day of her wedding to Jasper had arrived.

Grace fluttered around with excitement flushing her cheeks, no doubt envisioning her own impending nuptials, while Kitty went on chattering about the men of the ton who had caught her interest—and there had been many.

Hannah watched Elizabeth with a secret smile on her lips and her hand resting on the enormous bump of her belly, likely imagining Elizabeth in the same delicate condition that they might discuss children together and have them grow to be best friends as well.

In truth, the idea of motherhood was not unappealing. Elizabeth had never considered having a child before. Especially as she had never thought she would ever wed.

But imagining a child with Jasper's dark hair and dark eyes, how that small babe might look cradled in his strong arms, filled Elizabeth with a longing in her breast for a maternal bond that she was desperate to eventually know.

"After the ceremony, we need a moment alone together," Elizabeth warned her friends. "I have gifts for every one of you."

Lucy raised her brows. "I never say no to gifts."

But Jillian was skeptical. "Do I want to know what this gift is?"

A secret smile played over Amy's lips.

Elizabeth intentionally kept from looking at Hannah who was likely giving her a knowing smirk. "You'll find out soon enough. For now, it is time for this wallflower to break her vow and finally wed."

The others left the room in their lovely pastel dresses, leaving Elizabeth alone with her father to make their way down to the small chapel.

"Are you happy, Elizabeth?" He asked.

"I am." She took his proffered arm. "He loves me for exactly who I am."

Papa patted her arm. "You deserve nothing less. Your Mama always wanted you to rush into marriage so she could have grandchildren, but I told her to be patient, that your time would come. When the right man who was worthy of you came along."

He sniffed and Elizabeth looked up to find his eyes

watering with quiet affection. She pressed a kiss to his cheek. "Thank you for believing in me."

"Always, my girl. Always."

They walked down to the chapel, a small room on the first floor of the manor house, a relic from a time long before the newer portion of the home had been built around a medieval tower keep. Bunches of tulips adorned the short row of pews, and all of her family and friends turned when she and Papa entered.

But it was not her friends she saw when she made her way down the aisle. It was Jasper, appearing handsome in a dark jacket and breeches, his hair mussed in that way that was slightly out of fashion and just tempting enough for her to want to run her hands through.

His eyes lit when he saw her, a wide, unabashed smile lighting his face. His gaze swept down her gown, an elegant pale-blue silk with small white flowers embroidered at the hem. A gown her mother had ordered for the season in the hopes of securing Elizabeth a husband.

And now she had one.

She strode forward, not looking at the ground, too fixated on the man who would soon be her husband. The carpet underfoot caught on the tip of her toe, and she tripped.

Papa shot her a look of shocked horror, but Jasper only smiled wider, his expression endearing.

Rather than heat with embarrassment and humiliation as she might have done in the past, Elizabeth chuckled and shrugged her shoulders. After all, tripping was a natural part of her life, and she was done feeling ridiculous for every spill and stumble.

Her father handed her to Jasper, who thanked him, and together she and Jasper stood before the priest.

"I love you," Jasper mouthed. "You look beautiful."

At that, her face did heat, with pleasure at his words. With the knowledge that what he said was true. That he loved her exactly as she was, someone who would never chide her clumsiness or roll their eyes at her novels. But he would be at her side to hold her upright and read those very same books.

And be the hero in her own true love story.

EPILOGUE

The wedding breakfast was being assembled as Elizabeth pressed a kiss to her husband's lips.

Her husband!

The word was one she could not stop repeating in her head.

"I can't wait to find out who is next," Jasper chuckled, knowing full well what Elizabeth intended to do with her friends.

"I'll let you know."

"I'll wager it's Jillian."

Elizabeth laughed. "She'll hate you for saying that."

Jasper caught Elizabeth in his arms, filling her senses with that spicy, sensual scent so perfectly his. "I can't wait until I'm alone with you again, wife."

"Nor I, husband." She dragged a finger down his cravat and kept going until she curled her fingertip in the edge of his breeches. "There is still so much to explore."

And explore they had, for the night after Jasper's arrival, then the night before their family arrived. They had spent the evening before the wedding apart—for propriety—and it had been the longest night of Elizabeth's life.

"Soon." Jasper kissed her a final time, his lips full of promise, then he departed as he shot a wicked look back in her direction.

If the night before had been long, the day leading to that evening when they could be alone would be interminable.

Elizabeth gathered the four small boxes, one with a green ribbon for Hannah and pink ribbons on the others—each containing a small gold bracelet within—and went up to Hannah's room where her friends waited. The bedchamber was sumptuously appointed in brilliant sunshine yellow, befitting the brightness of Hannah's personality.

"Thank you to all of you for coming to my wedding. It wouldn't have been the same without all four of you at my side." Elizabeth hugged each in turn, careful with Hannah to avoid her bump. "This is a little something to express my gratitude."

Jillian held her pink-ribboned box like it was a snake. "I don't want to open it."

"Oh, don't be so silly," Hannah chided, pulling the green ribbon off hers and opening the box.

Amy did likewise and they both exclaimed at the same time.

"It's lovely," Amy said happily, and withdrew the delicate gold bracelet.

"Well, that is not what I thought it would be," Lucy said with a relieved laugh, and opened her own box.

Elizabeth held up her hand, revealing her own gold bracelet, a smooth chain with a five-petaled flower charm dangling from it. "This way the wallflowers can all match."

Jillian visibly relaxed as she opened her gift. "And here I thought you would be giving us bits of paper to see who would be next to marry."

"Oh, I did." Elizabeth grinned at them. "Look under the lid of your box. I went with the same system Hannah had used when she was the first wallflower to break our vow. Stars for the women who are not supposed to wed yet, and a heart for the one that is."

Lucy and Jillian both groaned.

Amy dutifully lifted her lid. "A star."

Lucy and Jillian groaned even louder.

"I have two connected hearts," Hannah exclaimed.

"I confess, I gave you that one on purpose since you're already wed," Elizabeth admitted. "There is one left with a single heart."

Lucy rolled her eyes and looked at the underside of the lid. "A star," she said with relief.

"I don't want to play this game anymore," Jillian hedged.

"It's you," Hannah cried. "You're next!"

Jillian sighed and flipped over the lid to reveal a perfectly drawn heart.

"It's just a silly game," Elizabeth rushed to reassure her. Considering how long Jillian's father had pressed her toward marriage, the last thing she wanted was for Jillian to feel forced to the altar by her friends as well. "You truly don't need to find love next."

But Hannah grinned and tapped her fingertips together. "Or does she? Who will be the next wallflower to break the vow?"

They all looked at one another in their wedding finery,

each assessing the other. For surely one of them would come next…and would it really be Jillian?

Whoever it was, Elizabeth only hoped her friends would find a happiness as true and as pure as she had found with Jasper. For no matter the vow, every wallflower deserved to be loved.

Want more? Check out my newsletter signup for a free download of *Her Highland Beast*!

A man destined to die, a woman who cannot be killed, and a curse that can only be broken by true love…

Go to <u>https://BookHip.com/NMAQCHV</u> now to get your copy!

A Ghostly Tale of Forbidden Love

The Madam's Highlander

Her Highland Destiny

The Highlander's Untamed Lady

Matchmaker of Mayfair

Discovering the Duke

Unmasking the Earl

Mesmerizing the Marquis

Earl of Benton

Earl of Oakhurst

Earl of Kendal

Heart of the Highlands

Deception of a Highlander

Possession of a Highlander

Enchantment of a Highlander

Standalones

The Highlander's Challenge - N W M S

Her Highland Beast - N W M S (fairytale twist retelling - Beauty and
the Beast/Princess and the Pea with Scottish folklore)

ABOUT THE AUTHOR

Madeline Martin is a *New York Times, USA Today,* and International Bestselling author of historical fiction and historical romance with books that have been translated into over twenty different languages.

She lives in sunny Florida with her two daughters (known collectively as the minions), two incredibly spoiled cats and a man so wonderful he's been dubbed Mr. Awesome. She is a die-hard history lover who will happily lose herself in research any day. When she's not writing, researching or 'moming', you can find her spending time with her family at Disney or sneaking a couple spoonfuls of Nutella while laughing over cat videos. She also loves research and travel, attributing her fascination with history to having spent most of her childhood as an Army brat in Germany.

Check out her website for book club visits, reader guides for her historical fiction, upcoming events, book news and more: https://madelinemartin.com